FIC
ROB

T5-DHH-927

Robinson, Jeanne.
Wild Flowers

WITHDRAWN

MAR 0 0

Fulton Co. Public Library
320 W. 7th St.
Rochester, IN 46975

WILDFLOWERS

WILDFLOWERS

•

Jeanne Robinson

AVALON BOOKS
NEW YORK

FIC
ROB

Robinson, Jeanne.
Wildflowers

© Copyright 2000 by Jeanne Robinson
Library of Congress Catalog Card Number: 99-068456
ISBN 0-8034-9403-3
All rights reserved.
All the characters in this book are fictitious,
and any resemblance to actual persons,
living or dead, is purely coincidental.
Published by Thomas Bouregy & Co., Inc.
160 Madison Avenue, New York, NY 10016

3 3187 00149 1709

PRINTED IN THE UNITED STATES OF AMERICA
ON ACID-FREE PAPER
BY HADDON CRAFTSMEN, BLOOMSBURG, PENNSYLVANIA

23 FEB 00 BOUREGY 10.47

Chapter One

Meg closed the suitcase and turned to face her roommate. "You don't think that I *want* to go back, do you?" she said. "I just don't see that there's any choice."

"There are lots of choices, Meg, but this might not be the best time to make them," Julia said. "You're in shock. Anyone would be whose parents were just killed in an accident, and the fact that they were driving down for your graduation makes it ten times worse. You shouldn't be making decisions now at all." Meg sobbed harder, and Julia gave up trying to comfort her.

Meg straightened up and reached for the box of tissues. "I have to go home, Julia. I have to go home and make funeral arrangements, and then I have to *stay* there and sort out their belongings and sell the house. . . ."

1

"Others could do that for you. You could hire some-one to close out the house. I wish we could come with you now so that we could help."

"And miss your graduation?"

"I would, if my parents hadn't already arrived. If I thought it would get you back here sooner."

"Well, it wouldn't. I've made up my mind, Julia. I want to take my time going through Mom and Dad's things. Then we'll see."

"What about your job? Will they hold it open for you? You can't just walk away from your first job!"

"Let's not argue about it now, Julia," Meg said as she started to cry again.

Meg was quiet on the bus to Vermont as she re-treated into her thoughts. She hadn't been home since Christmas. Then the woods had been white with snow. Now the rivulets rushed down the sheer rock faces that lined the roadside, gathering force as the last of the snow melted from the highest peaks. In the city spring had been present in all its lushness, with summer just around the corner. Here the spring seemed as fragile as the tiny buds that made their first, hesitant appear-ance. She took a deep breath of the cold, clean air. It never ceased to amaze her that a three-hour ride from New York City could make her feel as if she were on another planet.

She couldn't remember ever before using her key to open the darkened house. The tears started again. She was sorry that her brother would not be there until morning; she didn't really want to spend the night alone in the house that held so many memories. It would have helped if she had managed to arrive in time to pay a visit to the funeral parlor. She knew that the real force of the disaster would hit when she actually saw the bodies. At least John would be there with her then.

Meg touched each piece of furniture tenderly as she wandered around the house. She opened the old songbook on the old piano's music stand, and used one hand to pick out the notes of one of her mother's favorites. "Galway Bay" brought new tears to her eyes. Her parents had planned a trip to Ireland for later in the summer, sort of a celebration of the last of the college tuition payments. Meg pictured her father and brother standing with her around this piano as her mother played. She closed the cover over the keys.

She'd have to decide what to sell, what to keep. And in order to decide what to keep, she would have to know what she would do next, where she would live. A New York apartment, shared with others, would have very little room for this overly large, ornate, Victorian furniture with which she had grown up.

She felt the friendly presence of her family in every room of the house. There were long-ago memories: her grandfather in that chair, her grandmother puttering in the kitchen as she stirred the applesauce in that large pot. From more recent years she remembered her mother at the sewing machine in the spare bedroom, her father as he read the morning newspaper at the kitchen table.

She climbed the staircase and forced herself to go into the bedroom her parents had shared. She could remember when her father and mother bought this "new" bedroom furniture, when the contents of an old estate had been sold. She ran her hand over the carved headboard, admiring the workmanship. She could never sell this to strangers. Tears spilled over and ran down her cheeks.

She picked up the book that lay open on the bedside table. *Whose woods these are I think I know*, she read, probably as her mother had read on the night before their fateful trip. Her mother had loved Robert Frost's poetry, claiming that it reminded her of their own Vermont land.

Meg wandered into her brother's old room. Her parents' original bedroom furniture had been given to John. This furniture would be stylish forever, with its clean, almost Shaker, lines. She wondered if he might want it now for her nephew, Tommy.

She continued her tour. The memories of all the happy times served as a catharsis. Healing tears streamed down her face. She picked up the corner of the handmade quilt on the bed in her room and held it against her cheek. She had lost her parents, but she would have the wonderful memories. Some people had less than that.

Meg awakened in the morning as she heard the car pull into the driveway. John and Pam and Tommy and Judy were here. Meg had planned to be up long before this. The sun streamed in the window with the soft, pale light of early spring. This was to have been her graduation day.

Her brother embraced her silently. Even the kids were subdued. It seemed strange to be in the same room with John without indulging in some light banter. She knew that they'd get back to that later, after they had each dealt with the grief. Her tears began again as she turned to fill the coffeepot. Pam held out a grocery sack. "I brought doughnuts," she said. "I didn't think any of us would feel like cooking." Then she added, as if she had just remembered the suddenness of the deaths, "Though I'm sure there's cereal in the cupboard, and maybe even milk in the fridge."

Pam found a plate for the doughnuts. John grabbed one, and poured himself a cup of coffee. "We'll go down to the funeral home as soon as you're dressed, Meggie," he said. "I spent some time on the phone yesterday, so some things are already taken care of. I've made arrangements with him for the funeral, day after tomorrow. I called the newspaper so that they could run the announcement of the viewing. But there's still a lot to do."

She was barely listening. *Meggie.* It seemed so strange to hear that again. It had been John who gave her that name. He couldn't say Margaret, and so her parents had reluctantly settled for Maggie. But he couldn't say that either. It always came out Meggie, and the name had stuck. Not so bad, really. By the time she was a teenager she had become Meg, to everyone except her brother and her parents and their friends.

Meg drank the scalding-hot coffee. Her stomach rebelled at the thought of a doughnut. "I'll be ready in ten minutes," she called over her shoulder as she headed up the stairs.

She was lost in thought again as she stood at the mirror in her room and combed her long black hair. She could almost see her mother's reflection behind her, could almost imagine the hands that used to braid that hair as the two of them stood in front of that mirror. She blinked back the tears again.

Her usually pale skin was even whiter than usual, and she pinched her cheeks to bring some color to her face. She hadn't bothered with makeup, so the tears flowed from the blue eyes and down her cheeks without leaving a track, and the thick black lashes left no dark smudges when she wiped them with her fists as if she were still a child.

Meg went through the viewing at the funeral parlor in a daze. Her parents had lived in this little town all their lives and had known most of the other residents. Little old ladies with what John called dandelion hairdos hugged her. Families from their neighborhood knelt together to pay their respects in front of the closed coffins. Friends stopped to whisper at the wedding picture propped on the easel. Meg heard several say that they remembered the day that her parents had been married.

Meg wore the only black dress she owned, the latest in New York chic. She had thought that she would wear it at least once a week at the gallery. Now she wondered if, after the funeral the funeral the next day, she would ever wear it again.

The line of her parents' friends seemed never-ending. They kissed Meg's cheek and told her that she could call on them if she needed them. They promised to be at the church the next day. They told John that he looked more and more like his father every day, and that Tommy and Judy were the spitting image of the long-ago John and Meggie who had grown up here.

Half a dozen of the closest family friends came back to the house after Meg and John and Pam had said their good-byes to the last of the funeral home's visitors. They brought coffee cakes for breakfast and cookies for the children. Meg told herself that it was a good thing she'd decided to stay a while, because there were casseroles for at least a week or two.

At last the children were in bed and the visitors were gone. Meg was ready to collapse from the strain of the last two days. She sat down at the piano, almost too tired to play. The songbook was open, and it seemed that her fingers found the chords by themselves. Pam and John came and stood next to her. Three voices sang, subdued but in perfect harmony:

" 'If you ever go across the sea to Ireland . . .' "

It was a graveside service that could have graced the pages of a mystery novel. The cold spring rain came down, striking the opened umbrellas with its staccato pounding. The sky was gunmetal gray.

Meg's great flowing cape, which looked simply dashing on the streets of New York, here looked as if she should be running across the moor toward some Heathcliff-like lover. She knew that her parents' friends must be commenting on her clothes. But she also knew that the folks who had come to pay their respects last night and were gathered here at the gravesite today had known her since she was a child, and knew that she wasn't trying to show off. *Julia says*, she thought, letting her mind drift, *that at five foot nine and a hundred and twenty-five pounds, I wear my clothes like a fashion model. She tells me that the clothes I find in New York City's secondhand shops, like the cape, look as if they'd been made especially for me. But what I needed for this funeral—and don't own—is a perfectly ordinary raincoat. Never mind,* she thought. *It isn't a fashion show. The neighbors won't be fooled by my New York clothes. Everybody here knows that I'm still the same Meggie Ryan.*

She was still their Meggie, and she knew that they would all come back to the house after the graveside service, bringing comfort along with enough food to last her for a month.

"Well, Meggie," John said as they sat around the kitchen table after the last of the friends and neighbors had gone, "I can stay another day. I'll help you go through the house tomorrow, after we see the lawyer about the will. I don't think there's a new one since we all talked last. You know that you get the house— lucky you—and I get the insurance."

Her mind drifted off as she thought about the house. It was built in the twenties. Its kitchen had last been updated when Meg was a child. Her dad had talked for years about more insulation, but the money had gone for college for her and for John. Now, just as the tuition bills had finally reached an end, so had her parents lives', with all their hopes and dreams.

She tried to tune into what John was saying. ". . . there's enough food here to last several weeks, Meggie. You won't have to shop at all while you're here. Maybe we should decide what to do with it all. You can't take it back with you on the bus."

That brought her back to reality. "I'm not going back," she said. "That is, I'm going back to get my things, but then I'm coming back here. I'll take my time in selling off the furniture—whatever you and I don't want—and I'll stay until the house is sold. So I'll be happy to have all this food, John. Unless you want to take some home with you, it can just go in the freezer. I won't have to cook for a month."

"What do you mean, you're staying here? Are you crazy? I thought you had a job lined up. In fact, I thought that you were supposed to start next week. I thought you'd signed a lease on an apartment."

"Well, you're right. About the job and the apartment, I mean. Those are the major things that I have to take care of when I go back to town. But there are three or four other women who had wanted to room with Sharon and Julia. And the gallery owner won't have a problem in finding someone to replace me. Two thousand art history graduates are probably converging on New York City even as we talk."

"Meggie, what will you live on? I don't mean to be crass. But you're a brand-new graduate, and you're turning down your first job. What I'm trying to say is, I really don't need the insurance money. I was just going to put it in the kids' college fund. If you need it . . ."

"You think *I'm* crazy, but you're willing to fund me with your kids' college money? That's real brotherly love. Thanks, John, but I think I can find a job. I was a super waitress at the college's black-tie dinners. I can apply for jobs that say 'experience needed.' Besides, what I really want to do is paint. And I can do that here as well as in New York. Maybe better."

"You may be able to paint as well here, but I thought that you needed to *show* in New York. I thought that working in the gallery was supposed to be a way to make contacts. I thought—"

She interrupted. He was reminding her of what she knew to be true, and she didn't want to hear it right now. "New York is only three hours away, John. And I have friends there." Meg bit her lip, and he stopped in mid-sentence. He recognized that signal, one he'd seen many times as they were growing up. It meant that the discussion was at an end.

Chapter Two

Meg folded her clothes and piled them on the bed. She was surrounded by boxes, some empty and waiting, others already stuffed with the accumulation of four college years. She and Julia and Sharon had just moved into this tiny apartment during the week after final exams. Now she was moving out. She would load the never-unpacked boxes into her car and take them to be shipped by UPS. Then she'd stuff the little car as full as she could for the drive back to Bennington.

John had helped her decide on the car, a five-year-old with four-wheel drive, just right for Bennington's winters. He'd even written the check to pay for it. Well, she'd repay that loan quickly enough when she found a job.

She folded another sweater and tried to tune back in to what her roommate—no, her *ex*-roommate—had been trying to say to her.

11

"But I thought that working in the gallery was going to be a way to make contacts. I thought that they might even show your work themselves. I . . ."

Had all of her friends and relatives rehearsed the same lines? She changed the subject. "Listen, Sharon. I really feel bad about leaving you two. But I know that six of our crowd are still on a search for apartments, so you won't have any trouble in replacing me."

Sharon waved her hand in dismissal of that last comment. "I wasn't thinking of us, Meg. You're right. We won't have any trouble finding someone to take your place. We might even wait a month. If Julia and I both find jobs right away, we wouldn't mind having the extra space all to ourselves. I was just really concerned about you. I thought that you had big plans for things you were going to do and see in the city now that you aren't a starving student anymore."

"I'll be only three hours away. I'll have to bring my paintings down, if I can arrange to show them, so I'll be here once in a while for a weekend. I assume you'll let me have what would have been my bed—or that I can bunk on the couch if you do decide on a third roommate. Besides, even if I were here, I'd be at work all day and I'd be painting on evenings and weekends. I wouldn't have time to run around like a tourist."

"Will you look for a job in Bennington?" Julia asked. "Are there galleries?"

Meg smiled. This roommate had never been out of the city, unless you counted the vacation flights to London and Paris. Meg would have to make sure that Julia came up to Vermont for a weekend and see what country living was like.

"Actually," she replied, "there *are* some small galleries. There's a college there, with a really good art program. I might have considered doing my studies there instead of at NYU, except that I wanted to live in the dorm, away from home—and I wanted to be in New York. Anyway, lots of Bennington College graduates seem to settle down right in town. Bennington is kind of an artsy community. But most of those who stay in town are struggling. They run their galleries by themselves, or as a team. I don't think they're looking for extra employees. I'll look around, but I expect that I'll be flipping hamburgers at the Blue Ben. Though maybe, with all this high-class waitress experience that I have, I'll get lucky and be hired by the Bennington Station." She smiled as she thought of the two extremes represented by those eateries. She knew that her friends couldn't picture the two establishments in the way that she could, not until they came up for a weekend and saw what her little hometown was like. "Remember, I won't need much money. The house is paid for. The taxes are minimal. I'll have to earn enough to put food on the table and coal in the furnace and to repay John for the car. That's all. And if I'm waitressing, some of the food will probably be on the house."

"What if you sell the house right away?" Julia still wasn't ready to give up.

"Then I'll come back, and sleep on your couch, and look for another job. Or maybe I'll just look for an apartment and paint until I run out of money—I'd have the money from the sale of the house—and *then* look for another job. Maybe by the time I run out of money the paintings will sell, and then I won't need a job. Really, Julia, I can't think that far in the future. I can't spend my time making one set of plans for what I'll do if the house sells in a month, and another set for if it takes a year. I just have to take it one day at a time."

"And what about Erik?" Sharon asked. That was the question that they'd all been avoiding.

"We'll see," Meg said after a long pause. "There wasn't really anything definite. . . ." Her voice trailed off as she thought about Erik. They had so much in common: their love of concerts and ballets and theater, all the things that New York had to offer. And then there were the things that they *didn't* share: their views on money and politics, for starters. And the bigger problems, the ones that seemed to have no solution. Meg wanted children; Erik wanted to live in the city, unencumbered by anything more than a working wife. They'd discussed marriage, but so far only wound up telling each other why it wouldn't work. Unless a miracle happened, and Erik changed. . . .

"If he were *mine,*" Sharon said, "I certainly wouldn't leave him here to run around loose while I went off to some little town miles and miles away from the city."

"He's not exactly 'mine,' " Meg said. "Anyway, I'll be back here in New York often enough. Maybe some time apart will help us see whether we're meant to be together."

Her two friends walked her to where her car was illegally parked. Meg realized how her lifestyle had already changed. She had never had a car in New York, but of course it would be a necessity in Vermont. Sharon kicked the snow tires. The car was five years old, but the tires were new. "You haven't lost your north-woods smarts during your four years at school in the city," Sharon said approvingly.

"Remember, the two of us will be up for Fourth of July weekend," Julia said. "Try to arrange a parade or something."

Well, you've done it, Meg said to herself as she guided the little car over the Tappan Zee bridge. *You've burned the New York bridges behind you.* For a moment she felt all alone. She'd left Erik and Sharon and Julia. She'd abandoned what would have been her first professional job. Her parents were gone. They'd had dozens of friends in Bennington, but, aside from a few elderly women Meg knew from the neighborhood, there were none that she would call close friends of her own. She fought back a feeling of panic. This was her choice, and she was certain that it was the right one. She told herself that several more times, until she was finally convinced that she meant it.

June was not the time to be looking for a job in Bennington. The tourists came mostly in the fall to see the leaves, and in the winter to ski. The college was pretty much closed for the summer, except for a writing institute and a summer program for high school students. But both of those groups stayed on campus, unlike the regular students who ate a fair number of meals in town, so Meg knew that she was lucky to be hired even part time at the Blue Ben. She thought of Julia, who had probably never seen a real, old-time diner.

She suspected that the proprietor probably didn't

need her at all. But she had worked there during her high school years, and, like most of the people in town, he remembered her and had known her parents. Well, she was in no position to feel guilty about accepting a favor.

For the first week, all she did aside from work was sleep. She'd forgotten how hard a waitress/short-order cook actually works, even part time. She rushed from customer to customer as they sat along the long counter. She refilled coffee cups and cleared away dishes. She scrambled eggs and grilled burgers. She cut fat slices of homemade pies and topped them with ice cream. She made delicious concoctions with the old-fashioned milkshake machine. She dropped great scoops of vanilla ice cream into root beer to produce the popular root-beer floats. She relearned how to start the giant coffee urn and to refill it as the day wore on. She began to look back at her college days as if they had been one long vacation.

By the second week her muscles no longer protested. Her feet were tired at the end of her shift, but she bounced back quickly after a soak in the big old tub. Now her senses came alive, and she delighted in strolling through the pasture behind the house, seeing how many of the wildflowers she still knew by name. She walked to the river, still high from the spring runoff. She browsed through the galleries, not ready yet to try to become a part of the town's group of artists and art lovers, content just to know that she was not in a cultural wasteland. When the college opened in the fall, she knew that there would be plays and concerts and art exhibitions in the large gallery on campus. Despite what Julia and Sharon and Erik might think, she had not moved to the back of beyond. She knew that she would find friends with common interests, people who, in fact, managed to be more of a part of the art world than she was.

By the third week she had started to paint. She was not really surprised that her subject matter had changed to reflect her surroundings. The river, the wildflowers, the old bridges and mills . . . these were her new models. She painted as if to make up for the lost weeks, and canvas after canvas lined the perimeter of her sunporch studio.

She turned the calendar page. June was over. She remembered that Julia and Sharon would be here for the Fourth of July weekend. When they'd last talked on the phone, Meg had reiterated her plans—or, rather, her lack of plans. "First I'll sell the house, and then I'll decide what to do next." Now her friends would arrive in two days, and the house was still not for sale. The time had gone so quickly. Well, she needed a FOR SALE sign up right away if she didn't want them to know how she'd procrastinated. They'd report back to Erik, too. He assumed that the house was for sale, and she hadn't told him otherwise. She reluctantly admitted to herself that he had barely entered her mind. Oh, she had spoken to him on the phone a few times. But she hadn't missed him in the way that she had expected. Perhaps when she saw him again all of her old feelings would return in a rush—along with all of the problems that they couldn't seem to resolve.

She reached for the phone book and called a realtor. And then, so it would look as if she was prepared for prospective buyers, she carefully hand-lettered a sign saying MUCH OF THE FURNITURE IS ALSO FOR SALE.

PLEASE INQUIRE. She propped the sign next to the door from the sunporch to the parlor. There. Sharon and Julia would think that she'd been serious about this all along.

Chapter Three

They watched the parade from a vantage point in front of the old hotel on Monument Avenue. The high school band strutted proudly toward the monument, where a large vat of lemonade awaited. Julia and Sharon gazed at their surroundings. The ancient hotel was newly painted, its gingerbread restored to all its past splendor. Meg hoped that the owners would be successful in their venture, but she wasn't sure that the area could support one more antique mall. And if that's the kind of business that they wanted, then why not in one of the old factories that stood empty along the river? She answered her own unspoken question: she had met Rhoda and Alan, the young couple who were risking all their savings on the hotel. They were in love with this Victorian creation. If the antique mall didn't work out, they'd think of some other use for the old building.

The bells pealed from the tower of the little frame church, celebrating the birth of the nation. Meg prodded her friends in the direction of the monument, following the marching band that had just passed. She followed Julia's eyes as her friend studied the old houses that lined the street. Meg could almost read her thoughts—too bad that the house wasn't here, in the ritzy part of town. Meg could have sold it in a few days, or could have started some sort of bed-and-breakfast cum art gallery. Though some historic renovation was beginning on her side of the old railroad tracks, it would be a long time before Bennington was converted into anything but a workingman's town. The tourists visited in the fall, the skiers came in the winter, and all of the visitors thought that the town was charming and quaint. But, aside from a few Bennington College students who fell in love with the place and stayed on after graduation, there were not many permanent newcomers. In fact the population was gradually dwindling, as the local young people headed off for more exciting places to live.

"Nice of you to arrange this parade especially for us," Sharon quipped as the last row of tubas passed in review. "Now—where's the best place for ice cream? We may as well complete this Norman Rockwell picture."

"Grandma Moses, please! Our museum is filled with her work. We'll have to see it the next time you visit. Ice cream is down at the foot of the street." Meg reversed direction and nudged them against the flow of the crowd that followed the parade down toward the monument.

They sat in the old-fashioned ice cream parlor on

chairs with spiraled metal backs. They rested their el-
bows on the tiny round table as they sipped their
frothy ice cream sodas. "You're sure this isn't Norman
Rockwell country?" Julia asked. "I feel as if I've
stepped into a *Saturday Evening Post* cover."

Sharon leaned back in her chair and gazed out the
big, plate-glass window at the nearly deserted street.
"This reminds me of my grandparents' little town,"
she said. "I used to visit them when I was little. We
used to walk along the railroad tracks from Gram's
house to the drugstore in town to get chocolate malts."

"There hasn't been a train through here for as long
as I can remember," Meg said, "but the tracks are still
here, and there's a great restaurant in what used to be
the station. So I also remember walking the tracks.
Wait till we take the back way from my house to the
college. I think that rutted dirt road will remind you
of the days when you jumped from one railroad tie to
another."

Sharon was breathing hard as they made their way
back up the main street of the little town and turned
left toward where Meg had parked the car. "Out of
shape. No hills in the city," she muttered.

"It's level from here on," Meg said. And then, in
apology, "But there really wouldn't have been any
place to park in the center of town today. You saw
that."

"Climbing hills is probably good for us," Julia said.
"The hike relieves any guilt feelings about the ice
cream."

The three friends piled into Meg's little car. Meg
drove toward the edge of town. The sidewalks ended,
and, less obviously, streetlights were nonexistent.

Julia looked around. "Any nibbles on your house yet, Meg?"

Meg could see why Julia asked. Here, on the outer fringe of the town, there were five FOR SALE signs within sight. She knew that they would see three more before they reached her house. She gave a resigned gesture. "You see how it is. It's a buyer's market. Only there aren't any buyers." No need to tell Julia and Sharon that the house was listed only yesterday; it didn't matter anyway—some of these houses had been on the market for months. At least the realtor had put the sign up right away.

Last night, when Julia and Sharon had arrived, it had been too dark to look around. And this morning they'd been in too much of a hurry to get to the parade. Now it was time for the house-and-garden tour.

The house was built of local stone, an unprepossessing square relieved only by its two-level porch that stretched across the front. The lower porch had been glassed in, in deference to the Vermont winters and even the chancy springs and fleeting summers. Rocking chairs and an old porch swing still graced this first-floor level, just as they had when the porch was open. A few pieces of white wicker completed the picture.

They climbed the outside stairs to the upper porch, roofed over but still open to the weather. Here were three huge chaises, snug in their canvas wraps, protected from the evening dew. Meg pulled off the canvas. "Lemonade here in the sun?"

Julia nodded, and collapsed gratefully onto one of the huge lounge chairs while Meg went back downstairs to get the drinks. "I still can't shake the feeling that I've walked through a Norman Rockwell painting, never mind that this is Moses territory," Sharon said. "Lemonade on the second-floor porch. High school bands parading to the monument. Sun porches and ice cream sodas. It's certainly a good escape. What you should do," she said as Meg walked out on the porch with the tray of icy glasses, "is move back to the city to work, and come up here every weekend. You said the house was paid for. It shouldn't cost too much to maintain."

"That's a thought," Meg replied, carefully staying noncommittal. They sat and sipped and looked out toward the Green Mountains, still covered in mist. But the sun was high, and Meg knew that the mist would burn off by noon and that the mountains would be etched sharply against the sky. She breathed a deep sigh of contentment as she snuggled down into the cushion of the chaise. She was relaxed in a way that she'd forgotten during her years in New York.

She gave her friends a quick tour of the house, and then they headed outside to explore the yard. There was a garage of matching stone, with a loft above. They climbed the stairs. "What a great studio this would make," Julia suggested.

Meg looked around her with new eyes. The loft had been a playhouse for her and John, and then later a place to hold parties with dozens of teenagers. Finally it served as a depository for unused furniture. She'd forgotten about the things stored here. She'd have to haul them down, clean them up, find spots in the house where they could easily be seen by prospective buyers. She hadn't thought of using the loft. "With a ten-room house to myself," she responded, "I haven't exactly been looking for extra space. But you're right; it would be a great studio. It just needs some enormous windows in that north gable. And a bathroom, and maybe a little kitchen . . . maybe I'll be lucky, and a whole colony of artists will decide that my house and garage are just what they've been looking for."

She showed them the rest of the grounds. She pointed with pride to the flowerbeds, with Shasta daisies tumbling over themselves and daylilies crowded from years of division. They walked in the meadow beyond the garage, and she told them the names of the midsummer wildflowers—fleabane and bee balm and horsemint—as she gathered great masses of them until her arms could hold no more.

Meg arranged the flowers while Julia and Sharon prepared ham-and-cheese sandwiches. They carried their plates back to the upstairs porch, and Meg pointed out that the mist had flown away from the mountaintops. She felt as if time had slowed, that the whole town was still a part of the nineteenth century and that she was a part of it too.

"I wonder if I could get any work done here," Sharon mused, "or if I'd spend my days poking in the garden and gazing at the mountains."

"But Meg *is* working," Julia said, "harder than we've ever known her to. You saw the paintings propped in the sunporch. Her subjects have changed, but the style's pure Meg. I'd know it anywhere. You've got something special, Meg, with those fat, thick brush strokes that are your signature. It's interesting that you've switched from skyscrapers to mountains and waterfalls. And I like those wildflower attempts best of all. You should bring them down to the city."

"Gee, thanks, Julia." It really gave Meg a boost to hear her new work praised by one of her city friends. "I thought I would take some down in a couple of weeks. I owe the Blue Ben a lot of weekend work, after taking this one off. But I could manage to come down for a few days in the middle of the week."

"Do you want us to take a couple of paintings back with us on the bus? Your car won't hold them all."

Meg laughed. "And I probably won't be able to place them all, either. My best gallery contact, Diane Calloway, says that she'll take two for now. I'm glad she's not holding a grudge from when I backed out on taking the job with her. I'll bring my favorites when I go to New York, and we'll see what happens."

Julia looked out over the mountains, now silhouetted clearly against the cloudless sky. "I can't believe that it's so quiet. It's almost spooky."

Meg smiled. "Quite a change, isn't it? Wait till evening, when the night creatures start their songs. You've probably never heard frogs croak or crickets sing." She finished the last of her sandwich and stood up. "Bennington College art gallery, anyone?"

It was just a few blocks to the college. They tromped along the dirt road, then found themselves looking across a green lawn toward the music building. "The gallery's over there," Meg said as she waved her arm toward the huge modern edifice.

Julia picked up the conversation that had occupied them during their walk. "But aren't you bored?" she asked. Julia was a real city girl. She had tried hard to assemble a weekend's worth of casual clothes but still looked as if she should be strolling down Fifth Avenue instead of along a dusty road and through the meadow to the college's art gallery.

Meg tried for a serious consideration of the question. "I've been too busy to be bored. I've done a lot of painting, as you know. And Diane Calloway says that I can take two more to her each month, if she's sold the last two. She'd like to keep demand ahead of supply. And now I'll be dragging some of the furniture down from the loft. I'll get it organized for a garage sale in the fall, when the tourists are here. And I've been making lists of what's here, so that John can let me know what he'd like before I start to sell things. Plus, I work twenty hours a week at the diner. I could make it full time in September, but I don't think I will. I've managed to save money even at half time, and this gives me time to paint. Anyway, ask me again in the middle of the winter, when I've been snowed in for a week. I might be bored by then."

"But there are no shops—"

"Say, this is some place!" Sharon interrupted. Their hike had brought them at last to VAPA, Bennington College's enormous building devoted to the visual and performing arts. This tiny school had more performance space per pupil than any other in the country, and, during the school year, it sparkled from end to end with creative efforts. Now, with school out for the summer, the vast building seemed empty and cavernous. A small group of precollege students, here for a summer experience in theater, were hard at work in one room. A couple of students worked on sculpture. But the kilns were cold, and the enormous sprung dance floor was empty.

The threesome walked out onto an upper-level vantage point and looked back over the meadow in the direction they'd come. The great stone music building, the original mansion on this vast acreage, marked the boundary of he school property. Just to the right, a road meandered through the woods. At the near end of the road, a footpath skirted the rear entrance to the mansion. A few blocks further, but miles away in real estate value and sophistication, was Meg's house. She had strolled over to VAPA or to the music building often enough when she was in high school, to attend plays or concerts or art shows. In the fall, she knew that the college would once again become her cultural home.

The voice behind them interrupted Meg's memories. "May I help you ladies? Would you like a tour?"

Meg, with her artist's eye, took in every detail of the stranger even as she answered automatically. He was a several years older than she, perhaps around thirty, though his rusty-colored hair and beard made it hard to judge. He was tall and slim and moved with the grace of a dancer. She watched, out of the corner of her eye, as Julia shifted her stance as if suddenly conscious of her own posture.

Meg held out her hand. "Hello. I'm Meg Ryan. I don't really belong here, I guess, but I grew up in town and now I'm living here again. I wanted to show my friends the college. We were all art majors. Sharon and Julia live in New York."

He was really good looking when he smiled. "I'm Brian Davidson. I teach here, in the drama department. I guess you don't need my tour, Meg, if you grew up here and if you're an artist. You probably know your way around the building as well as I do. You're welcome, too, you know. We like to encourage good relations with what we call 'the townies.' "

"We'd like your tour," Julia chimed in. She tossed her red curls so that they fell attractively into place.

That girl is no fool, Meg mused.

"What part of the South are you from?" Sharon asked.

"You mean I can't claim that I've lost my accent? I'd have thought that six years of drama training and a dozen years in the North would have done it." He grinned. "North Carolina," he said in answer to the question.

"And the dozen years in the north?" Julia persisted.

"Six at Yale, long enough to get my BA and then the Master of Fine Arts degree. Six here, teaching at Bennington."

Meg did the calculation. Eighteen when he left home to go to college, twelve years since then. Thirty. It had been a good guess.

An hour later, even the ever-talkative Julia had run out of questions to ask. It seemed only polite to invite Brian home for dinner. Meg would have thought of that all by herself, even without the whispered prodding from Julia. He went off to make a phone call. "I'm all yours," he said as he returned, directing the comment at the three of them. "Take me home and feed me."

Brian looked appreciatively at Meg's paintings, stacked around the sunporch. "Good. Really good. Are you showing them anywhere? I have a friend with a gallery here in town."

"I've sold some of my stuff in New York, but the

wildflowers are a new subject for me." She didn't want to sound smug, so she added hastily, "But I'd love a contact here. As you can see, I'm turning out more than my friend in New York has room for in her showroom. I'd really appreciate any advice that you can give me about the local scene."

"Do you get down to New York?" Julia clearly wanted him on her turf, instead of here, helping Meg make local contacts.

"Oh, yes. I'm usually in New York for the summer, as a matter of fact. I have a standing offer to act as assistant director for an old friend whenever he's got a play on during June, July, or August. He usually has something, off-off-Broadway. This summer, though, it's my turn to teach part of the July program." He waved his hand back in the general direction of the college where the young students had been rehearsing a scene in the theater. "But I'll be in New York in January, for sure. Our students are off campus then, for their Fieldwork Term. Jerry Adams, my friend in New York, will probably hire one of them, along with me—maybe for a bit part, maybe just folding programs or working the ticket booth. Fieldwork Term is a wonderful opportunity for our students to get some real-life experience, though my private theory is that the school sends them off in January because it's too expensive to heat the buildings—especially VAPA and the music building."

He insisted that he help scrape the dishes and load them in the dishwasher. Julia managed to get his address and phone number, and scribbled down her own for him.

"Do you actually think he'll call?" Sharon asked

after he was gone and the three friends were back on the upstairs porch listening to the serenade of the frogs.

"Do you actually think I'll just sit back and wait? I have every intention of calling him sometime before Christmas. He'll need to be reminded that he has some new friends in New York."

Next morning Meg awoke with the sun, as the birds set up their morning riot outside her window. She slipped downstairs and started the coffee, and then walked out into the meadow to greet the day.

She reappeared in half an hour, rosy-cheeked from her exercise, arms again laden with wildflowers, this time brilliant blue cornflowers and saucy yellow daisies. She was surprised to see Julia at the table, newspaper open, coffee cup at her elbow.

Meg reached in the cupboard for a vase and plunged the flowers into the water with no attempt at arrangement. They fell into place, achieving the natural look that florists might slave to attain.

"We have to leave for the bus soon," Julia said, just as Meg said that they'd better wake Sharon and start breakfast so that the two New Yorkers could head back to the city.

"Two great minds with a single thought," they said again together and laughed.

Meg drove her friends to the station and waved good-bye as the bus pulled away. It had been a great weekend. Julia, at least, seemed to love the little town almost as much as Meg did—though perhaps meeting Brian had a little to do with that.

Meg brushed back a long strand of hair as she walked back up the front steps. A tiny thought was nagging at her, just at the edge of her mind. A whole weekend with her best friends, and no one had mentioned Erik even once. Neither Julia nor Sharon had asked how things were going with him. They hadn't nagged her about trying harder to sell the house, so that she could get back to New York and Erik. No one had told her that if she really loved him she would want to be with him all the time.

Chapter Four

Her friends' visit gave Meg the incentive that she'd been lacking. She spent some of her at-home hours deciding which of her paintings to take to New York. A few more hours were used to complete one that she particularly liked, a close-up view of some of her favorite wildflowers, the pink fleabane and some white daisies. She'd sketched that picture while lying almost flat on her stomach; the result had been worth it.

She also spiffed up the house a bit. She washed windows, polished furniture, and rescued some of the better pieces that were languishing in the loft and brought them back to the house. She tried to view the house as a prospective buyer might, and concentrated on producing that homey, lived-in feeling that someone retreating to the country should find irresistible. Her usual bouquets of wildflowers were supplemented with rustic baskets filled with things gathered in the meadow—milkweed pods, tall grasses, an interestingly shaped branch.

It was with mixed emotions that she finally drove her little car across the Tappan Zee bridge and reentered the world that she had left . . . when? It seemed like a million years instead of just a little over a month ago. She found herself caught up in the excitement of the city. And yet, she noticed the dirt and grime in a way that she never had before.

She drove directly to the gallery at which she was to have worked. She'd talked with Diane Calloway, the owner, by phone, and had a promise of some display space for a month. She wanted to unload the paintings before she did anything else. She had retained enough of her city smarts to know that she couldn't just leave the paintings in the car while it was parked on the street, and she saw no point in lugging them up the stairs to what would have been her apartment and then carrying them all back down again. Definitely the first stop had to be the gallery.

She stayed just long enough to discuss the hanging of her work, and for a little more polite conversation with Diane. She felt strangely out of place, here in this tiny gallery where she had anticipated spending her entire work week. She told herself that she'd feel better when and if some of her pieces actually sold. Right now she had relinquished her old role but hadn't yet made the transformation to a new one. Fortunately her escape was easy—she could justifiably claim to Diane that she was tired from the drive, and she could tell herself that she was eager to see Erik, that he would be expecting her, and that he would begin to worry if she didn't appear at his doorstep soon.

Fulton Co. Public Library
320 W. 7th St.
Rochester, IN 46975

Next stop, unloading her suitcase at the apartment that she was supposed to have shared with Julia and Sharon. They were both at work, but they'd promised to leave the key with the super. She wanted a chance to shower and change, and maybe a chance to collect her thoughts, before she drove the additional ten blocks to Erik's apartment.

She forced her mind to go blank as she stood in the shower, concentrating only on the warm water that cascaded through her long hair and down her back. This was not the time to analyze her feelings for Erik, or for New York City. She would relax and enjoy these few days, and save her introspection for when she got back to Vermont. Vermont seemed designed for solitude, for self-analysis. New York was for fast-paced, heady experiences, shared with friends and colleagues and sweethearts.

She toweled the long, dark hair and combed it straight down her back. Her Sixties look, her friends called it. She slipped into slim black slacks and an oversized Irish fisherman's smock, more thrift-shop finds. It would be hot by midafternoon, especially compared to Vermont, but somehow she didn't think that shorts would project her "New York look." She didn't want to appear as if she'd just arrived from the country, even though that might be the truth. She applied her makeup more carefully than she had for the last two months, and set off to disturb Erik in the midst of his work on the Great American Novel.

Actually, all she interrupted was a TV program that seemed to involve a stock-car race. She looked at Erik accusingly. "You're right," he said sheepishly. "I should be hard at work. Correction—I should have made it *look* as if I'd been hard at work. I need a half-typed page in the typewriter, and I should have hit the remote when I heard the doorbell."

"You'd never have fooled me, Erik. I know that you use your word processor. A warm TV and a cold computer mean goofing off. How do you expect to become the Sidney Sheldon of the Nineties?"

He winced. "You wound me, woman. Here I am, trying for James Joyce, and you accuse me of Sidney Sheldon." But he grabbed her and kissed her to show her that all was forgiven. "I've missed you more than I can tell you, Meg. Six weeks! It felt more like six months."

She clamped down on her thoughts. She'd promised herself. This was not the time to stop and think about whether it had felt like six months to her.

Julia was the one who was fascinated by Brian, but it was Meg who got the phone call, Wednesday night shortly after she got back from New York. "I ran into my gallery friend today," he said. "She'd like to see your paintings. When would be a good time?"

"I'm working tomorrow until ten. Friday?"

"Sounds good. She should be available Friday evening; it's not a late night for the gallery. But perhaps you'd like to see that, too?"

"Of course I would. When?"

"If you're free Saturday morning, we could do a tour of the shops in town, perhaps have lunch."

"It all sounds great, Brian. I'm not on at the diner until Saturday dinnertime. I'll see you here, then, Friday night." She hung up the phone with mixed emotions. It wasn't really a date—more like a professional contact. He was bringing a gallery owner to look at her paintings. Definitely not a date. It was just as well. She didn't know anything about him yet, except for the fact that he taught at the college. She remembered how much Julia hoped for a call from Brian, and added guilt to her other apprehensions. As she headed up to bed, she told herself again that this was merely a professional meeting.

She almost dropped the chair she was carrying from the garage loft when something warm and soft wound itself around her leg. She put down her burden and stooped to get a closer look at the small bundle of fur. "Aren't you a bit young to be wandering around by yourself?" she asked the kitten.

It followed her across the lawn toward the house. "Go home," she said. She carried the chair out to the sunporch. She'd need to work on removing some of the grime, but it looked like the type of item that would sell at her sale. She headed out to the loft to collect another. She tripped over the kitten, which went scooting off around the corner of the house.

When she headed out the door for work next morning, the kitten was sitting on the front step. It mewed plaintively. She hardened her heart and ignored it. It would never go home if she started to feed it. She'd planned to get a watchdog. She certainly had no intention of being adopted by a kitten.

It was waiting for her when she got home from work. "Mew?" It was clearly a question. She stepped over it and went in to prepare her supper. She peered out once to see it sitting on her front step.

She was just putting the supper dishes in the dishwasher when the doorbell rang, promptly at 8:00. Meg shook hands with Brian's friend, Liz Roberts. "It's okay if your cat comes in, isn't it?" Brian asked. She caught a glimpse of a white fur ball racing past them into the kitchen.

"It's not my cat. It's a cute little thing, though. I wonder why it's hanging around here. It must be hungry. I don't dare feed it, though, or it will never go home."

"It probably can't go home," Liz said. Meg looked at her questioningly. "It was probably dropped here. One of the hazards of living in the country. People drop unwanted animals on your doorstep, hoping that you'll take them in."

"You mean that it probably hasn't eaten since I first saw it yesterday morning?"

"That's likely. If you don't want it, though, Meg, there's an animal shelter in Williamstown."

"But I do. I didn't think that I did . . . I was thinking of a large dog. But I do." Meg reached down and grabbed the kitten and cuddled it in her arms. "The poor little thing," she said. She reached for the door of the refrigerator. "Fortunately, I have some hamburger."

"Just a little," volunteered Liz. "If it hasn't eaten in two days, something that rich will just bounce back up. Maybe you could mix it with a little cereal."

Brian stood back, amused. The kitten was the center of attention as Meg and Liz mixed a gruel of cereal, hamburger, and milk.

Finally the women had taken care of the kitten's needs to their satisfaction. The little cat was involved in attacking the mixture that had been prepared for it.

Meg caught Brian's eye as she straightened up from the task. He raised an eyebrow and smiled that wonderful smile. "Oh," she said, suddenly aware of just why they were here. "Oh. Liz wanted to see my paintings." The three of them burst into laughter together. The kitten had charmed them all.

"I like the wildflowers," Liz said after looking carefully and professionally at all of Meg's work.

The kitten had followed them into the sunporch, and was winding itself around Meg's legs. She stooped to pick it up, absentmindedly. "Everybody seems to like those," she said. "It's funny—that's a new subject for me. Of course, it helps to have them growing in my backyard."

"I could sell some of those, when the tourists start coming. I don't mean that like it sounded," she added hastily. "It's a professional gallery, if I do say so myself. But Brian said you grew up here, so you know that there's no money in the town. Gallery sales are to outsiders."

Meg nodded. "I knew what you meant. I'm looking forward to seeing the gallery. I'll be coming by tomorrow morning." She glanced at Brian for confirmation.

"Brian said that he was giving you the grand tour." It was said casually. Meg had hoped for some clue as to the relationship between her two guests, but she couldn't read anything in Liz's words.

"Coffee?" She remembered her role as hostess. They accepted readily, and the cat led the way back into the kitchen.

"Have you thought of a name yet?" Brian asked, as he helped her set out mugs and spoons.

"The dog was going to be Fang," she replied. "I guess that's not appropriate." The small creature picked that moment to stop scrubbing itself with its little tongue. It stretched luxuriously. A large yawn revealed tiny white teeth.

"I think it likes the name," Liz said. They all joined in the laughter. The kitten had found a name.

"Next is the Bennington Potter, and then Liz's gallery is just another block up the street." Brian was giving Meg what must be his standard tour. He showed Bennington to her just as if she hadn't grown up right here in town. She enjoyed seeing her hometown through new eyes, from the view of someone who had chosen to live here instead of just being born in town.

They browsed through the salesroom of the Potter, one of the oldest pottery makers in the country. It was, of course, not new to Meg. Her family, like most in the area, had been drinking their coffee out of mugs classified as "seconds" for as long as Meg could remember. The showroom was crowded with tourists who had arrived in town at the first late-summer nip in the air with hopes that the leaves would already be brilliant red and orange. *Way too early,* Meg thought, but she was pleased for the local merchants who would profit from the disappointed leaf-gazers.

Meg felt a sense of keen anticipation as they headed up the street to Liz's gallery. She studied the little shops here at the crossroads of the town. She hadn't been on this street in years.

Very modern . . . that was what struck her as soon as she walked into Liz's gallery. *Liz must concentrate on showing the works of recent (or even current) Bennington students,* Meg thought. *I wonder why she would want the wildflowers—they're so different from everything else in here.*

Liz came in to meet them. She wore a basic little black dress, nearly a clone to the one that Meg had thought would serve her in such good stead at her own gallery job. As if she had read Meg's mind, she said, "You're must wonder why I want the wildflowers, when everything else is so avant-garde. I *need* the wildflowers, Meg. Half of my potential customers turn tail and run almost as soon as they walk in the door, deciding that my tastes are not theirs. I have quite a classic selection of jewelry, and yet that isn't what hits you as you come in. I need some striking pieces of a different style from the works that my friends on campus are producing. I'd like to be showing a whole spectrum of art. Your works would be a good start."

Meg nodded, satisfied, already too caught up in examining the art to carry on much of a conversation. "You have some good pieces here," she finally said.

"Thanks." Liz turned toward Brian. "I can close up any time," she said. She reached for the sign that she'd hang on the door . . . OUT TO LUNCH. So it was to be a lunch date for three. Meg reminded herself that she had always meant it to be a business meeting.

The Brasserie seemed to be transplanted out of New York's Greenwich Village. Its sunny room and rough-tiled floors gave it a rustic air, and its menu was pure *nouvelle cuisine.* All of the city's sophistication was here, in this little town in the Green Mountains. The residents who were involved in the arts read the *New York Times,* drove down once a month to visit the

galleries and museums and see a play, and then re-
treated here, away from the bustle of the city but still
in touch. Meg was reminded again that this was a business luncheon when Liz extracted a contract from her
oversized purse and read out the salient points.

Meg read the contract and signed her name. She ate
her grilled tuna slowly, savoring every bite. Brian insisted that they have dessert, and when Meg saw the
chocolate mousse she gave up her protests. They lingered over coffee. Brian rambled on about how he
always looked forward to the fall term. "It's like a
fresh start once a year," he said. "I can't imagine a
job like yours, Liz, with no beginning and no end."

"I see an ebb and flow at the gallery," she protested.

"Ebb and flow is not the same as wiping the slate
clean. I can have a horrible Shakespeare class—not
that I ever do—and know that next term they'll be
gone, replaced by a whole new bunch of students."

"We used to say exactly that same thing about our
courses and our professors," Meg said. "It's amusing
to hear it from the other side of the desk, so to speak."

Liz picked up the check, smiling at Brian as she
said, "Business expense, Luv." Meg and Brian promised to bring three paintings back to the shop that afternoon.

Meg and Brian were carefully loading paintings
from the sunporch into the backseat of his car while
trying not to trip over Fang, who was winding himself
between their legs. Meg tried to sound casual. "Have
you known Liz long?"

"Four or five years. She was one of my first students. Bennington's art majors often dabble in drama,
and vice versa. Talented young lady. There was never

any doubt in her mind, though, that she wanted to own her own business. She even took advantage of our cross-registration with Williams to take the business courses that we don't offer. She's not at all interested in producing the art, though she could if she wanted."

That didn't really answer Meg's unspoken questions about their relationship. Not that she cared, she added to herself.

Next time Julia and Sharon came up, she'd show them Liz's gallery, with her paintings prominently displayed.

Chapter Five

It was several days later when she saw Brian's car turn in to her driveway from her vantage point in the backyard, flat on her stomach as she sketched more wildflowers. She scrambled to her feet and brushed the dirt off her jeans. Fang bounded along behind her as she headed to the front of the house.

"I just finished my grocery shopping, and decided on the spur of the moment to drive over and see if you were home. I thought that you might like to make a trip to the Humane Society, to look at dogs."

Meg could barely focus on Brian's words. The little boy in the child seat in the back of the car held her attention. His rusty hair matched Brian's. He looked at her with enormous blue eyes.

Brian followed her gaze. "Meg," he said, "this is my son Michael. Say hello to Meg, Mike."

The child removed his thumb from his mouth, muttered something that sounded a little like "Hi, Meg," and put the thumb back in his mouth again.

How old was he? Meg tried to imagine him next to her brother's children. Three, she guessed. "How old are you?" she asked. Michael proudly held up three fingers, and Meg nodded, congratulating herself on her guess.

And where was Mrs. Davidson? Home with a red-haired baby? No, that couldn't be true. Brian wouldn't have come for dinner when Julia and Sharon were in town if it meant leaving a wife at home with two small children. Divorced? That did seem more likely. Probably he had child visitation rights on the weekend. A visit to the Humane Society would be good amusement for the little boy.

She told herself to stop inventing possible lives for this man. She tried to remember what Brian had been talking about.

"Humane Society. Dog," he repeated.

"Dog," Michael echoed, temporarily removing the thumb.

Meg wiped some more dirt onto her jeans. "I'm not sure that I need a dog, now that I've got Fang."

"I think that you do. It gets pretty lonely here in the winter. And the area has changed a little in the past few years, like everywhere else. It's no longer the type of town where no one locks the house. And even with the new security consciousness, we get one or two break-ins a year. And you're really out here on the fringe of the town, Meg. I'd feel better about your being here alone if you had a dog."

"And if I sell the house next month, and move back to a New York City apartment?"

Brian looked at her as if he couldn't believe she'd do that. "Houses aren't selling very fast," he said. "Of course the dog could always make another trip to the Humane Society." She looked aghast until she saw that he was joking. "Been looking for a dog myself. I could hold off, till we see what needs to be done with *your* dog." He sounded as if this dog were a foregone conclusion.

"What if Fang is afraid of dogs?" She was trying to be a part of this bizarre conversation, when what she really wanted to know was more about the child . . . or the wife.

"How could he be, with a name like Fang? Seriously, Meg, that's why I think you should do it now. Fang is young enough to adjust to anything. He hasn't caught on yet to the old enmity between dogs and cats."

"Maybe a *small* dog," she agreed. He ushered her into the car before she could voice any more objections.

She was not a small dog, but her big, sad eyes captivated Meg. And she was not a puppy. Six years old, as a matter of fact. Her elderly owners had reluctantly decided to move into an adult care complex. And so Meg found herself adopted again, this time by a Saint Bernard named Brandy.

"Meow!" screeched Fang, as he scrambled up the stairs and leaped under Meg's bed. A deep *woof* was the response from Brandy.

"Ignore them," Brian suggested. "They'll be friends within a month. Meanwhile, the house is plenty big enough for them to keep their distance."

"Coffee?" She glanced at the old schoolhouse clock that hung on the kitchen wall. She took a deep breath as she settled on the image of father and son on their own for the weekend. "Or maybe an early supper? I was planning to make spaghetti." She turned to Michael, who had abandoned his thumb in favor of petting Brandy. "You like spaghetti, Michael?"

" 'Getti," the little boy said. "I like 'getti, Meg."

Brian ruffled his son's hair. "I should get back to work. I'm writing a play. Jerry, my friend in New York, will consider putting it up this winter if I finish it by September. But Mike and I can never resist spaghetti. What can I do to help?"

She set Brian to work preparing the salad (with a little help from Michael) while she browned the meat. She grabbed a jar of home-preserved tomatoes from the shelves that lined the cellar stairs. She had enough of these reminders of her parents to last about a year. Then she'd have to resurrect her mother's recipes and start a garden of her own . . . if she was not back in New York. It was surprisingly easy to forget that her stay here was supposedly temporary, just until the house was sold. She set the sauce to simmer. She checked the cupboard and found a bottle of Evian water. She put it in the refrigerator just to give it a little chill, even though she'd be pouring it over ice. In the chest-type freezer in the large pantry that adjoined the kitchen, she found a loaf of her mother's homemade bread and took it out to thaw. There were only a few loaves left, but her mother had taught her how to make bread. She'd warm this loaf in the oven when everything else was ready.

She stirred the sauce and added spices. She poured glasses of iced tea for Brian and herself. She handed Brian some crackers and a small plastic glass of juice for Michael, pleased at his nod of approval as he saw that she understood the needs of a three-year-old. "We've half an hour or so until it's time to start the pasta. Want to sit on the porch with this?"

The dog followed them to the porch and flopped at their feet. Michael downed his juice and then sat down next to the dog. He cuddled against the soft orange-and-white coat while he stuffed crackers in his mouth. His rusty-colored hair nearly matched the dog's fur.

Before long a small white bundle of fur could be seen, its pink nose peering over the frame of the screen door. Brandy raised her head, and Fang scooted off again. Michael laughed. "Curiosity will win out. You'll see," Brian said.

Brian and Michael fed the dog. Meg lit the oven of the old gas stove so that she could warm the bread. She put the water on to boil for the spaghetti. While she waited, she set the table. Neither she nor Brian made any attempt at small talk. The silence between them was easy, comfortable.

She tossed the spaghetti into the boiling water. Brian refilled their glasses. One more glass of juice kept Michael happy until the pasta was done.

Brian and Meg filled their plates at the stove and carried them to the table, along with a smaller bowl for Michael. Brian cut Michael's spaghetti into manageable pieces and spread a slice of bread thickly with butter. "It's good, Meg," Michael said. "Bread's good. 'Getti's good."

Brandy flopped across Meg's feet. "She'll be handy as a foot-warmer in the winter," Brian quipped. "To Brandy," he added as he raised his glass.

"And Fang," she countered. "My little family is complete." She paused. "Tell me about *your* family, Brian."

"Car accident," he said. He stared at his plate. "Laurie skidded on an icy road, and the car went over the side of the mountain. A year and a half ago." He paused as if it were too difficult to go on. "She was four months pregnant."

Meg put her head in her hands, reminded of her parents' accident such a short time ago. But at least they had lived long, good lives. She looked up at Brian and then over at Michael. She didn't know what to say.

Brian stared at his plate again, then raised his eyes to meet hers. She could see his pain. She wanted to reach out and hold him, but there was a look his eyes told her that he didn't want her pity. She guessed that he could talk about it only if he looked at it as something that had nothing to do with him—that he had to shove it away, keep it at a distance.

"My next-door neighbor cares for Michael," he continued. He sounded as if he were reciting the facts by rote. "Her husband Jason teaches biology at the college, and Angela is, for now, a stay-at-home mom with two children. Robbie is Michael's age, and Carrie is just a baby. Michael and Robbie will be in nursery school three mornings a week next fall. I'm sure that Angela can hardly wait."

"Nursery school," Michael interrupted. "Michael and Robbie go to school." It was the longest sentence

Meg had heard him say, and she smiled as she recognized that he was getting used to her a little.

"Michael was accustomed to being at Angela's house," Brian continued in the same detached voice. "Laurie went back to work as a nurse in the local hospital when he was just a few months old. So at least that's one thing in his life that didn't change."

"And you," Meg said, nearly in a whisper. "That makes two things."

"And me," Brian acknowledged as he draped his arm around his small son. He changed the subject. "Has Liz hung any of your paintings yet?"

At least he doesn't drop in there every day, she thought, *or he would know the answer to that question. Not that I care*, she added in her silent monologue, ignoring the fleeting picture of herself as a stay-at-home mother, caring for Michael and an unidentified baby, working on her painting while Michael was at preschool and the baby slept. She'd heard that young widowers didn't last long on the "open market"—that most women felt the urge to nurture and couldn't resist a man in need. That was ghoulish, she thought, and promised herself that she would not be one of those who rushed in to fill the gap left by the dead wife.

She realized that he had asked a question. "Yes," she replied. "Two of the wildflower pieces are really very prominently displayed. I feel fortunate to have them with her—and fortunate that you helped me make the contact. Thanks again."

"My pleasure, Meg. It's what I would have done for any of my students. Helping young people get started is part of my job."

Young people. He can't be much older than I am,

she thought. *I thought of him as a friend, not as a professor.*

She stammered a response. "I went to such a huge school. My professors hardly knew me, except for the artists who taught the studio courses. It's really hard to imagine the student/professor relationship at a school as small as Bennington."

He laughed. "Sometimes it gets tricky. There are always a few students who think that they're madly and eternally in love with me. It's hard to maintain the balance between a close mentorship and something that crosses the boundary of professional ethics. Sometimes I have to give a gentle push before a little bird will leave the nest."

He's warning me off, she thought. *He's telling me that he's willing to help me professionally but that he doesn't want to get involved.*

She stood up to clear the table. "Coffee?" she asked.

"Better not," he said as he glanced at his sleepy-looking son. "I really have to get back to work on my play. I'll help you with the dishes before I leave, though."

"Dishwasher," she reminded him. She waved her hand in the direction of her favorite kitchen appliance. "No work involved."

"Well, then," he said. He seemed, just for an instant, lost for words. "I should get Michael tucked in for the night and then get back to work. I hate to eat and run, but I feel guilty enough as it is when I think about ducking out on the writing."

"No problem."

He stood at the door, somehow awkward in his good-byes. "I don't know when I'll see you next,

Meg," he said. "School starts in a couple of weeks, and I'd hoped to be finished with this play . . ."

"I understand." He was reminding her again that he didn't want to get involved. She met his eyes. "I'll be in New York for a few days anyway, and then I'm having company over Labor Day weekend. Thanks again for all your help."

Fang and Brandy wrapped themselves around her legs as she watched the car back out of the driveway.

Chapter Six

The city sweltered in the late-summer heat. Meg almost felt that the painted wildflowers in the backseat of her car had started to wilt. It had seemed pointless to worry about the little car's lack of air-conditioning on the damp, chilly spring day when she purchased it in Vermont. Now her stockings were glued to her legs, and her linen dress was crumpled.

She found a parking lot a long block away from the gallery. She tried to look cool and poised as she walked up the street. She stopped to mop the sweat from her brow. The wrinkles in her dress had mercifully disappeared thanks to the humidity, which Meg estimated at about ninety percent. Nothing like New York in the middle of August, she reminded herself.

She wondered why she had bothered to dress in her New York look. She knew that the gallery owner would not be there; Diane had escaped the city's heat, spending August on Cape Cod. There would be some new college graduate minding the store, whoever was lucky enough to land the job when Meg left it vacant. *Maybe that's it,* she thought. *I don't want my replacement to look down her sophisticated nose at me.*

"Sharon!" she exclaimed, as the slim salesgirl with the sleek blond twist in her hair turned to see who had entered the gallery. "You've got my job?"

"You didn't want it," Sharon said apologetically.

Meg hugged her. "You know that I didn't mean it that way. 'My job.' Poor choice of words. You know what I meant. This job is a plum, and there must have been lots of competition. You should be proud of yourself for landing it. I'm so happy for you."

"I've been here a month," Sharon confided. "I wanted it to be a surprise."

"Well, it certainly was. I almost dropped the paintings. Here," she said, thrusting the small canvasses toward her old friend. "I'm glad I don't do wall-sized works. I'm worn out from carrying these just a block."

"You could double-park, you know. The police don't bother people who are just unloading or loading. I'm glad you didn't, though. Now you don't have to run right off. Sit down and cool off. You can see that we're not exactly overrun with customers. I think that the city has been practically deserted this month. I'll get some coffee, and we can catch up on what you've been doing."

"There's not much to tell," Meg said as she settled back with her coffee. "I'm still working twenty hours a week at the diner. I'm still painting furiously. What's new with you?"

"And the gorgeous Brian?" Sharon asked, ignoring

Meg's question. "Julia spins fantasies about seeing him in January."

Meg felt the blush rise to her cheeks. "He's been very helpful," she said carefully. "He introduced me to a local gallery owner, who's sold one of my paintings so far and is very optimistic that she'll sell more when the tourists arrive . . . and he helped me pick out a dog." *And he's a widower, with a little boy who looks just like him,* Meg said to herself. She wondered why she didn't offer that information to Sharon.

"A dog?"

"A Saint Bernard. She thinks she's a lap dog. There's also a kitten . . ."

"You've really settled in. I thought that this Vermont thing was supposed to be temporary, until you sold the house."

"I don't know. I'm so happy there. I'm painting so well. And it's not all that far from here. Anyway, it's not as if home buyers are beating at my door."

"What about Erik?"

Meg bit her lip. The silence stretched for what seemed like forever. "I don't know about that, either. We'll see each other whenever I come down to bring paintings here. He'll visit Labor Day weekend. I don't know yet if that's enough to keep the relationship going or not. If we're really in love, it shouldn't be a problem."

"And there's some question of that?"

Meg bit her lip again. "I just don't know, Sharon," she snapped. "I'm heading over to see him when I leave here. You're asking at a bad time. I'm always filled with doubts when I haven't seen him for a couple of weeks. That was true whenever we were apart for college vacations, and it's true now. Ask me again when I get back to the apartment tonight, or at breakfast tomorrow morning." She stood up to leave.

"I didn't mean to hit a sore spot," Sharon said.

Meg stopped midway to the door. "I know that," she said. "I'm sorry that I snarled at you." She walked back and hugged her ex-roommate. "See you later at the apartment," she said. "It will seem like old times."

By the time Meg reached Erik's Chelsea apartment she felt truly bedraggled. Her conversation with Sharon had done nothing to improve her mood; she didn't want to think about how things stood between her and Erik. When she thought about it, she realized that their relationship was going nowhere. But here she was, in New York, ringing Erik's doorbell. She pushed the uncomfortable thoughts out of her mind and resolved to have a wonderful weekend.

"It's open," Erik yelled. She walked in to find him hard at work at the word processor. At least she hadn't caught him goofing off again. That would have been just too much on what had so far been a rotten day.

She leaned over and kissed him on the back of the neck. "Novel going well?" she asked.

"Novel not going well. I'm just trying to show you that I actually do work at it." He saved the file and turned off the computer. "Ugly weather, isn't it? I'm sorry that I can't offer you a tall glass of lemonade out on the porch—Sharon and Julia told me how you live a real country life. How about a glass of Perrier in the kitchen?" He kissed her tenderly. "I've really missed you, Meg. When are you going to leave the sale of the house to somebody else and move back here where you belong?"

She gritted her teeth. This was exactly the wrong way to start the weekend. She was already tired of being nagged about where she chose to live. *Chose* to live. Yes. She was ready to admit it. She had chosen to live in Bennington. She was not going to move back to New York—not ever.

It didn't seem like just the right moment to make that announcement, though. She smiled. "I don't know, Erik. The wildflower paintings are doing so well right now." She knew that was a snide comment, a reminder that his own work was stalled. She allowed herself another swipe. "I can't find wildflowers on the city streets, you know. And I'm really enjoying the cool summer."

"What about me? What about us? I hate being without you. I think that you must be my muse. I've always written easily, until now."

"Let's not argue, Erik. We have so little time together. It's a shame to waste it bickering."

"You're right," he said sheepishly. "I'm so glad to see you, and here I am giving you a hard time. I'm so proud of you, Meg. Maybe I'm a little jealous, too. Your work is going so well. You're selling your paintings. You seem so content."

He moved away from her to open the bottle of sparkling water. She followed him and wrapped her arms around his waist. "We'll have a wonderful time for the three days I'm in town," she said. "And then in less than two weeks it will be Labor Day weekend, and you'll have three days in Vermont. I've already booked you a room at Grandma's House. It's one of the nicest bed-and-breakfasts in town."

"You have a ten-room house and I'll be in a B&B? That makes no sense at all. Surely you can trust me to stay in one of your spare bedrooms!"

"It's a small town, Erik—one where everybody knows everyone else. My neighbors know that I'm living alone. If you stayed there with me, there would be gossip. I don't want that." They argued a little, but Meg stood her ground. "It will be all right. You'll see." She wondered whether her vague words were meant to convince him or to convince herself.

"How's Erik?" Sharon asked, greeting Meg as she emerged from the bathroom, towel wrapped around her long hair.

"Fine," Meg replied, trying for a smile.

Sharon looked at her, obviously waiting for something more.

"Everything's great, Sharon. It seems just like old times. Here I am, in the apartment that I planned to live in. I've dropped off paintings at the gallery that I planned to work in. I've watched Erik struggle with the novel that he's always planned to write." She shifted the topic of conversation slightly, away from any discussion of her feelings. She counted on her fingers as she ran through the litany of events they had planned. "Tonight we're going to the ballet. Tomorrow while he's at work I'm going to spend the day at the Metropolitan. Tomorrow night he has tickets to *Chicago*. Tuesday morning I'm going uptown to browse through the Cloisters."

"Sounds super," Sharon said.

"Yes," Meg replied. "In some ways it's as if I'd

never been away." She turned to pour herself a cup of coffee, trying not to think about her real feelings about what she'd just said.

Three days, she thought as she crossed the Tappan Zee bridge. *Three days, and in some ways it felt like three years. I can't believe that I ever wanted to live in New York. I'm rushing back to Vermont as if I can't bear to be away from it another minute.*

Brandy nearly knocked her over when she walked in the door, and Fang added to the attack by wrapping herself around Meg's legs. "Okay, you two," she said as she bent down to scratch the kitten's ears while being slobbered on by the big dog. "I'm happy to see you, too." Brian's prediction had been right on target. The animals were now the best of friends. They slept curled up next to each other on Meg's bed, down near her feet.

It's great to be able to hire one of the kids next door when I go to New York, she thought. *Kenny feeds these beasts and keeps an eye on the house too. Brandy would really feel cramped in a kennel. Of course I probably could have taken her to Brian's.*

As if on cue, the phone rang. "Have you been away?" Brian asked. "I've tried off and on over the past couple of days."

"Yes. I just walked in. Brandy and Fang are expressing their pleasure at seeing me. I took some paintings down to the gallery in the city, and spent three days with Sharon and Julia. You remember them." *And Erik,* she thought. *I wonder why I've never mentioned him to Brian.*

"Sure," he said. "The sleek blond and the bubbly redhead."

"They'll be glad to hear those descriptions," she said. She suspected that Julia would be happy to be remembered at all.

"I called to see if you'd like to go to a concert. You know that the Boston Philharmonic spends the summer at Tanglewood. This is their last week. I was thinking of tomorrow night."

"Oh, Brian, that sounds super. I haven't been to a concert since I graduated and left New York."

"Well, then. I'll let you get unpacked and get back to your appreciative animals. I'll pick you up at about seven tomorrow night."

"Would you like to come to dinner first? We could eat at six."

"Liz is coming, too. I'm sorry; I didn't make that clear."

Well, I should have realized, she thought. "I'd enjoy having Liz come to dinner, too," she said quickly. "I'll call her myself to issue the invitation."

I've missed hearing live music, she thought. *Erik and I will have to go to a concert when I go down to the city next time. Concerts and plays and ballet and museums—the New York experience. He'll take the opportunity to remind me once again of all the things I'm missing; he'll enjoy that.*

She glanced at Brian, sitting between her and Liz. *It's nice to have such good friends,* she told herself. *I'm lucky that they've included me in their lives.*

Brian caught her look and put his hand over hers,

squeezing it gently. She knew that that just meant that he hoped that she was enjoying the concert. She squeezed his hand in reply, and then put her hand demurely back in her lap. Her fingers tingled strangely, as if she'd just touched a live wire.

Meg was first to be dropped off. Brian walked her to the door. His hand touched her shoulder. "You seemed enchanted by the music," he said, carefully meeting her eyes.

There was that tingle again. Meg forced herself to hide her emotions. "It was wonderful," she said coolly. "Thank you for including me."

She held out her hand for the usual handshake. He took it in his, but bent over to kiss her lightly on the cheek. "Good night, Meg. I'll call you, probably after Labor Day."

Meg stumbled in the door. *It was a friendly gesture,* she told herself. *We're all good friends—we can't keep shaking hands. That's all it was—a friendly gesture.*

"This is a really great town," Erik said as they finished their tour of Williams College and headed off for lunch at the Williamstown Inn. "Lots of old money here. Why don't you try to place your paintings with some gallery here?"

Meg glanced back toward the campus, with its gray stone buildings that clearly showed their nearly three hundred years of age. "It's old, all right. Nearly as old as Harvard. How about some of those dorm rooms, with the wood-burning fireplaces!"

"The paintings, Meg."

"Oh. Yes. Good idea. I'll see if anybody at the college has any contacts. I think that some of Bennington's faculty even teach a course here occasionally. I know that the students can cross-register; the two schools have had a really close relationship ever since the days when it was Williams men and Bennington girls."

He looked annoyed. "Why not just bring a couple over here and make the rounds?"

"I could. I'd just rather do it my way." She bit her lip.

If he remembered the unconscious signal, he ignored it. "Try it both ways. Young artists need every trick in the book to become established."

"I'm doing all right, Erik. I make enough money."

"You make enough money to live here. You don't make enough to come back to New York. You don't even make enough to give up slinging hash."

"I'm enjoying myself, Erik."

This time the icy glint in her eye was too obvious to miss. He reached across the table and put his hand over hers. "Peace. I was only trying to help." He reached for his water glass with his free hand and raised it in a toast. "To painting sales—wherever they may occur."

She smiled, though it seemed forced. Still, Erik's attempts to get her back to New York came as no surprise. He'd been all too ready with similar suggestions when she was in the city last. But, of course, he was just trying to help her carry out their original plan. She really shouldn't be annoyed.

"Two more weeks," he said as they lingered over dessert at The Brasserie on his last day in town. "You are coming down again in two weeks, aren't you?"

"You know that I am. See if you can get some tickets for another play, will you? And maybe something at Lincoln Center. Isn't it your job to make sure that I'm not culturally deprived?"

"Good idea. The arts should be really back in full swing starting next week. The summer's over."

"When you come up next, the fall foliage should be at its peak. I'll keep you posted; sometimes it's early, and sometimes it's late."

He reached over and covered her hand with his. "I come to see you," he said, "not some colorful trees. You'll be back in New York two weeks from now. I'll be here again a couple of weeks after that, whether the trees are at their peak or not."

Chapter Seven

"Do you like your job at the Blue Ben?" Brian asked casually. He sat in the big rocking chair in the sunporch and watched Meg put the final touches on a painting of cornflowers. Michael played at their feet, building a tower of the colorful blocks that Brian had brought to keep him amused.

Meg looked up. "I like to eat," she replied with a smile. "I feel lucky to have the job at the Blue Ben. I know that they didn't really need me during the summer, but with the students back at the college I'm finally earning my keep. It's ideal, Brian. It's only half time, so I still have time to paint. And yet it provides enough money for my needs." She turned back to her painting. She chewed on the end of her paintbrush in concentration as she studied her work.

"I just wondered . . ."

She looked up again. It hadn't been just a casual

question; he had something on his mind. She put her painting out of her mind and waited for him to continue.

"I saw a notice on one of the VAPA bulletin boards. An announcement for an assistant in the art department. It wouldn't pay as much as waitressing, though."

Meg sat back on her heels. A job at the college . . . what a fascinating idea. "But they'll be looking for someone with at least a Master's Degree, won't they?" she asked.

"No, not for this. Actually, even some of our faculty don't have advanced degrees. Bennington is more interested in what one has written, or painted, or produced—at least in the arts areas. When you become internationally famous, we'll hire you for a teaching position with just that BA. In the meantime, you're probably exactly what they need for this assistant's position."

"But there must be a dozen Bennington graduates still in the area who would be even better suited."

"No. They'd be exactly what we wouldn't want. Inbreeding is a bad idea at any college, and at one as small as Bennington it would be fatal. Our students need to see a variety of techniques from a variety of sources. That's why you'd be perfect. Not only is your degree from a reputable institution, but you've experimented with a few different styles already. The wildflowers certainly don't look anything like those canyons of skyscrapers that you did before you moved up here."

Moved up here. She still hadn't really thought of it that way. It was supposed to be temporary, just until she sold the house. This news of the job opening at the college forced her to reevaluate her intentions.

"Do you really think I'd have a chance?" She could already imagine it. It sounded perfect. It sounded like just what she'd always wanted, even though she hadn't known it until just this minute.

"I wouldn't have mentioned it if I didn't think you'd be qualified." He pulled a piece of paper out of his pocket. "Here. I wrote down all the details. You can think about it, at least."

She began to believe that it might be possible. "Oh, Brian, I don't need to think," she said. She got up to give him a hug. "I'd love it. Thanks for thinking of me." She kissed him impulsively on the cheek. "Of course," she said as she sobered a little, "applying isn't getting."

"I'll keep my fingers crossed for you," he said. He scooped up Michael and the building blocks. "Time to get back to work instead of just watching you, delightful though it's been."

He turned as he reached the door and added, in what seemed like an afterthought, "How about dinner Friday night? Out, I mean; I wasn't hinting for an invitation for Michael and me."

"I'd love to."

"Seven?"

"Great. See you then."

"With Liz, I suppose," she said to Fang after his car pulled away. "Not that it matters, of course."

"You did *what?*"

"Applied for a job at the college, Erik. I should know about it sometime next week."

"What about selling the house? What about moving back to New York? What about me?"

She put her hand out to touch his arm. "I don't see that this changes anything. You know that I haven't even had a nibble on the house. You know how well I've been painting since I've been in Vermont. If you'd thought about it at all, I think you'd have realized that I might stay there for a while."

"A while. A while had an end to it. It sounds as if you've decided to stay forever."

She bit her lip, her signal that she was sick of the argument. "I haven't been offered the job yet, Erik. Let's cross that bridge when we come to it. Come on . . . it's been nearly a month since I've been in the city. What bit of cultural rejuvenation do you feel I need most?"

"I've got tickets to the ballet. Lincoln Center." He still looked sullen.

"Wonderful," she said, trying to sound enthusiastic enough for two. She looked at her watch. "I'd probably better be getting back to Julia and Sharon's pretty soon to change, if we're eating before the performance. What time shall I be ready?"

"All of you—you and Julia and Sharon—need to be ready by seven. They really wanted to see this ballet, and we all thought it would be fun for you if we all spent an evening together. We decided to eat after, though, so you still have a little while." He reached for her and pulled her toward him. "Come here, Meg, and tell me how much you've missed me."

She watched the dancers as they pirouetted gracefully, and yet her mind was not really on the action on the stage. This was a big night out on the town, and she wasn't really very excited about it. She'd been pretending that it was important to get down to New York once a month—and this weekend was forcing her to realize that it really wasn't very important at all.

She clapped automatically as the curtain fell, trying to show more enthusiasm than she really felt. She summoned up a smile, trying to look excited and ready for the next stage of her night in the city.

"I got the job!" *And I should be calling Erik,* she thought belatedly, *and not Brian. Still,* she rationalized, *it was Brian who told me about it. It makes sense for him to be the first to know.*

"Congratulations! Michael and I will be right over with the champagne. It's chilling in the refrigerator—how's that for confidence?"

It was probably only fifteen minutes later when the doorbell rang. Meg was aware of a pang of disappointment when she saw Liz next to Brian on the doorstep, but she quickly forgot the feeling as she was enfolded in bear hugs and kissed soundly by both of her visitors. Brian waved the champagne bottle recklessly. He seemed almost as excited about the news as she was.

"This is so perfect, Meg," Liz said, after the initial excited greetings were over and the toasts were was done. "You'll really feel like part of this community of artists now."

"And that means that it's time to get rid of that dratted sign," Brian announced impulsively as he headed down off the porch. He tugged the FOR SALE sign loose and tossed it with abandon over to the far side of the driveway.

What will Erik think? Meg questioned. She looked over at Michael, who was clinging to Brian's leg. She looked at Brian and Liz, who were still on a high because she got the job. She was conscious of a feeling of peace, secure in the knowledge that the right decision had been made.

"Here, like this," Meg said. She leaned over to help the new freshman mix the pigments. This was really fun. Many of the Bennington students arrived with their techniques already perfected, looking only for a nurturing place to work while they found their own style. But there were plenty of students in the art classes who had never painted before, taking advantage of the college's encouragement to try new things. And these fledgling painters were happy to have whatever hints Meg could give them. It made her feel almost like a real teacher, instead of just an assistant.

The faculty had also made her feel welcome and needed. She had dropped into place here at this little college as if she'd been here always. How, she wondered, had she ever convinced herself that she wanted to live and work in the city?

The students began to gather up their brushes and start their cleanup. Meg glanced at the clock on the wall. How nice to have a job like this, in which it was only some outside stimulus that made you look up and notice that the day was half over. Nearly noon. She'd been working with these students since 9:00.

As if on cue, Brian poked his head into the studio. "Lunch at the Commons?" he asked.

"Great. I'll be ready in a few minutes." He knew her schedule. Tuesday—another class this afternoon, but time enough in between for a quick lunch on campus. Mondays and Wednesdays she worked just in the mornings; sometimes they met Liz for lunch in town, and on some days she and Brian collected Michael from his neighbor and took him out for a burger.

"How's the play going?" she asked, between bites of her tuna sandwich.

"Which? The one the students are producing here, or the one I'm presumably writing?"

"Presumably? Maybe that answers my question."

"It does. I'm really stalled. My characters won't come alive."

"Maybe it's the weather." She looked out over the college lawn toward the mountains in the distance. The trees were really at their peak now. "It's hard to sit inside at a word processor when the weather's so nice."

"Could be. At least your craft demands that you spend the good days outdoors, sketching. Maybe the play will fall into place in a couple of months, when the weather turns nasty."

November. Yes, November can be nasty. She'd forgotten.

Brian and Michael had come for lunch. Now Brian was putting the remains of the cold chicken back in the refrigerator and loading the dishwasher. Michael wanted to play with Brandy, but the big dog was sound asleep in the sunbeam that came through the kitchen window. Fang was nowhere in sight.

Meg tried to figure out how to amuse Michael. If

this became a regular event, she'd have to forage in the attic to see what old books or puzzles or toys might be stashed there, remnants of the happy childhood that she and John had spent in this house.

She wondered if Michael would enjoy some music. "Piano?" she asked. He looked puzzled. She took his hand and led him into the living room. She folded back the lid over the piano keys and hit a chord. His face lit up. She took his hand in hers and picked out "Chopsticks" with his chubby little finger.

She let him sit on the piano seat and bang on the keys. When he tired of that she sat down next to him. She opened the old songbook. Brian came and stood next to her, and his clear baritone rang out as she hit the opening chords of "Sidewalks of New York." She joined him, picking up the harmony with her strong alto voice. Michael looked from one to the other, fascinated with this new game.

Meg lay awake in bed that night as sleep refused to come. She tried to think of Erik, but her mind kept returning to Brian. She reminded herself that Brian belonged to Liz. She rolled over, then back again. She apologized to Brandy and Fang for the disturbance. Brandy heaved a sigh as she settled back down across Meg's feet.

"You were right," Erik said. "These trees are really something! You're painting them, aren't you?" He settled back with his lemonade on the second-floor porch and looked out over the mountains.

"You'd better believe it! Diane wants two as soon as I can get them to New York."

"At least this new job leaves you with weekends free," he said, "so when you do come down to the city I'll be off work and will be able to spend more time with you. And you'll have a long Christmas vacation. Maybe this won't be so bad after all."

"I really enjoy the job," Meg said. "It's hard to imagine that I might have been selling other people's works at Calloway's."

"But it's just until May, right? What happens then?"

"This contract is just until May. But I should know before then whether it will be renewed for next year. I think the college is pretty pleased with me."

"You mean this job might be permanent? I figured that in the spring you'd put the house back on the market and look again for a job in New York."

"I don't know how you could have thought that. I have the dog, the cat—"

As if on cue, Fang jumped in Meg's lap. "The dog and the cat," Erik said with a sneer. "They're more important than I am. Why do I always feel as if I'm last in your life, Meg?"

She bit her lip. There was no point in starting this discussion now, when he'd be leaving in less than an hour to go back to the city. She'd had good intentions of telling him, during this visit, that their relationship was at an end. Somehow she hadn't found the right time. Maybe this was a good time. He'd be upset, but he could just get in his car and leave. No, she didn't want him to drive back to the city while his mind was on her, thinking of the relationship that had just ended. The memory of her parents' automobile accident was still too fresh in her mind.

*   *   *

The sky was gray and bleak. The trees, so lovely just a couple of weeks ago, had shed their finery during yesterday's fierce winds, except for some brown leaves which clung to the oaks. The autumn colors lived on, though, in Meg's sunporch, where she was putting finishing touches on half a dozen paintings of tree branches captured at their peak. She had promised four of them to Liz. "Too pricey for the tourists, Luv," Liz had said, "but they will entice them into the shop and help me sell *something*. And, who knows, maybe we'll even sell one or two."

The other two would go to the New York gallery. The wildflowers were gone, both from the garden here and from the walls in New York. All but one had sold. That one, Diane told her, would reemerge from the gallery storeroom at the first hint of spring, waiting to capture the buyer who couldn't wait for the end of the drab winter.

I suppose I'll do snow scenes next, Meg thought. *Why not? If they were good enough for Grandma Moses, they're good enough for me.*

The telephone interrupted her reverie. She always felt a thrill when she heard Brian's deep, mellow voice.

"Would you like to go to New York with me next weekend?" he asked. "I've got to have a discussion with Jerry about January term, and we'll get more things settled face-to-face. I know that you haven't been to the city in about a month, so you must be planning a trip to take some paintings down. I thought we'd both enjoy the drive more if we did it together. Mike is spending the weekend at Angela's, so I'll be a footloose bachelor—and feeling only a little guilty at having a weekend to myself."

There was a long pause. Meg's mind was racing. His idea made perfect sense, and yet . . . . She had, so far, managed to keep her New York life separate from her Vermont life. If she went to New York with Brian, the illusion would be shattered. He'd expect her to see her city friends. He would even expect to see them himself, at least Sharon and Julia. She'd never even mentioned Erik. Incredible, when she stopped to think about it.

"Meg, are you still there?"

"Umm. Yes. I'm sorry, Brian. The idea sort of took me by surprise."

"Well, that's certainly clear. Funny—it seemed so logical to me."

"It *is* logical, Brian. It's a super idea. When did you want to leave?"

Now it was his turn to hesitate. "Friday after class. But if you don't want to . . ."

She tried to sound confident. She'd work out her schizophrenia later, she told herself. "Friday's fine. I'll call Julia and Sharon and let them know that I'll be camping with them. Sharon can let the gallery know that a couple of paintings will be arriving. In fact, that's a good incentive to finish them up. That's what I was doing when you called."

"Great. I'll let you get back to it, then."

But "getting back to it" was not what she was inspired to do. She sat down heavily, welcoming Fang as he jumped up into her lap. "Well," she said to the cat, "I had to face it sooner or later. I certainly can't go to New York without seeing Erik, at least long enough to tell him that it's over. And I certainly can't go to New York with Brian without including him in our plans. Of course, he may have plans of his own; he may not be in the least bit interested in seeing my friends. But I'll have to make the offer. And, if he takes me up on it, I'll have to introduce him to Erik. And I'll have to decide why that thought upsets me so much."

She picked up the phone to call Sharon at the gallery. Her announcement was greeted with squeals of excitement. "You're coming to New York with that hunk? Wait till I tell Julia."

Julia. That's right. Julia was really impressed with Brian. Maybe she'd spend so much time gushing over him that he wouldn't have a chance to notice that she and Erik were presumably a couple . . . not, she reminded herself, that it mattered.

"Glad to do you all this little favor," Meg said. "Remind Julia, though, that I don't know his plans yet. He may have no time at all to spend with us."

"You'll have to insist, that's all."

Meg didn't want to insist. She was still hoping to keep her two lives separate. No need to tell Sharon that, though. "We'll see, Sharon," she said. "Don't forget to tell your boss that some autumn foliage will be coming her way on Friday."

Chapter Eight

Brian helped Meg load the paintings into the trunk of his car. She was not sure why she was surprised when he drove off in what seemed like the wrong direction for New York and came to a stop in front of Liz's gallery. Liz had obviously been watching for him. There was not even any need to find a real parking place as she stepped out of the door, suitcase in hand, turning the sign to CLOSED.

Meg instinctively began to open the car door, prepared to move to the backseat. "Stay," suggested Liz. "I'm going to sleep all the way to New York, so I'll be happy enough to stretch out in the back. You can have the job of making small talk, keeping the driver company."

And I was worried about having Brian meet Erik, Meg thought. *I'm a fool. Brian thinks of me as one of his students--his protégée—or, more likely, some stray, like Fang, who needs his protection. And I-I think that I'm in love with him. Or could be, if it weren't for Liz. If he'd ever turn my way. Whatever it is that I'm feeling, it certainly puts a damper on the way I feel—or felt—about Erik.*

Brian turned the radio to the classical station, softly, so as not to keep Liz awake. *He doesn't need my company,* Meg told herself. She turned to stare out the window, trying to work up some enthusiasm for this trip.

"You're staying with Sharon and Julia, aren't you?"

It was an opening that couldn't be ignored. "Yes. They were thrilled to hear that we were coming to the city together. They're hoping that we can all do something together tomorrow night." *Not quite true,* she said to herself. *Sharon and Julia can't be hoping to do something with Liz. But, of course, they didn't know that Liz would be coming. I didn't know that Liz would be coming, though I certainly should have guessed. Liz is always with us.*

"That sounds like a good idea to me. Maybe you and your friends would like to see Jerry's current play. It's in a loft, off-off-Broadway. He'd be thrilled to have three extra paying customers."

Was this the time to say it? She bit her lip. "Four," she mumbled. *Unless I face up to telling Erik goodbye before we go to the play.*

"Good. Four is even better."

He's not even curious, she thought. *I don't know why I was so worried.* She turned to look out the window so that he wouldn't see her bite her lip in an effort to hold back the unexpected tears.

"So," he said, after what seemed like forever, "who's the fourth?"

Good grief. She'd just finished being upset that he showed no interest, and now she had to face up to something even more upsetting—that he *was* curious, and that she really did have to tell him about Erik. *Well, maybe not very much about Erik,* she thought. *Something, though, and soon. I must seem like an idiot, unable to find the right words.*

"His name is Erik," she said, finally.

"Ah." He waited.

"We'd been seeing each other in college. We still keep in touch." There. That was at least partially the truth, but she felt the blush rising. She bit her lip. It wasn't going to help this time, though. Even if Brian knew that that was her childhood signal to end a discussion, there was no way to cut this one off at this particular spot. She wondered if he could tell just how uncomfortable she was. She stole a look, sideways, through her long black lashes. He was grinning. He knew that he had her on the spot, and he was enjoying himself.

"He's convinced that New York is the only place where one can be creative," she said finally, steering the conversation away from what part Erik might play in her life. "I'm trying to show him how wrong he is."

"You should have him come to visit. Bring him over to the college, Meg. We'll show him creativity!"

"He's been up . . ."

"Ah—the Labor Day visitor."

She felt caught, but she knew that anything she said next would just dig her hole a little deeper. Perhaps he was willing to change the subject. "Julia and Sharon were really excited about seeing you again." There. That should do it.

"I thought they'd be up for another weekend by now."

"They had hoped to get up while the foliage was at its peak, but Sharon can't seem to get any time off from the gallery. They've really been busy this fall. That's good for her, though; she won't have to worry that they'll decide that they don't need her. It's good for me, too. I'm always happy to see the gallery busy, especially when they're selling my paintings."

"Your Erik . . . what does he do?"

"He's not *my* Erik. We're just friends." She tried not to feel guilty at the outright lie. Just friends, who once in a while discuss marriage. Just friends, although she wouldn't be seeing him anymore. Well, she had committed herself now. "He works for a publishing house, and tries, in his free time, to write the Great American Novel."

"Too bad he's locked into nine-to-five. I don't think I could write under those conditions. The college has a great writers' workshop every summer, though. Maybe he could use his vacation to do some serious work on his writing."

Meg thought about that. "I'm not really sure that he's serious enough about it to spend vacation time on it," she said as she thought how little writing he had accomplished—maybe none actually—since graduation.

They were getting near the city, and the traffic was beginning to get ugly. *Thank goodness*, she thought. *Brian will have to concentrate harder on his driving.*

He won't be able to ask any more questions, at least for a while.

Brian slowed for the sharp curve of the exit ramp, and Liz began to stir. "Almost there?" she muttered, as her curly-haired head emerged over the back of the seat.

"Just off the expressway. You could sleep for another half hour. Maybe an hour, with this traffic. I always forget how bad it is."

Meg gazed out the window. The streets were grimy. The sky was gray. The pedestrians hurried along the sidewalks. She could imagine frowns on their faces.

"It's great to be here, isn't it?" Brian asked. She turned toward him in amazement. His thoughts couldn't have been further from her own.

"You really like the city?" The surprise showed in her voice.

"Sure. Don't you? You're the one who almost became a permanent New Yorker."

"But that was before . . ." *Before what?* she asked herself. *Before I realized how much I thought of Vermont as home? Before I found out how well I could paint there? Before my job at the college? Before Brian?*

He interrupted her thoughts. "I couldn't stand it if I thought it would be forever. But I love being here every January, and I look forward to the occasional weekend at other times. When you know that it's temporary, this city is the greatest place on earth!"

"We'll go to your gallery first, Meg," Brian said. "It's in the Village, right?"

"Soho, actually. If you go down Broadway to

Broome and turn right, it's just a block or so down the street. But I hate to drag you so far south."

"Jerry lives in Tribeca. It's hardly out of our way. And where will you be staying? We can make that our next stop."

"Oh, no. I can't have you driving up and down the streets of Manhattan all afternoon. Sharon and Julia live in the East Village. You've already been helpful enough." She glanced at her watch. "I'll stay at the gallery and chat with Sharon and Diane until closing time, and then go home with Sharon. The subway at rush hour will make me feel as if I've truly come back—and remind me of how much I enjoy Vermont."

"What about this evening? We'll be going to the play tomorrow night—I'm still assuming that you and your friends are interested—but tonight I think we'll just be hanging out at Jerry's apartment. Would you like to come along?" He arched a bushy eyebrow. "All four of you?" He turned partially around to the backseat. "Liz, write down Jerry's address and phone number for Meg." He turned back to Meg. "You and Sharon could just come along now if you want. It seems silly to trek north and then back south again."

"I think it would be better if we all came down later," she muttered. She thought of Julia, sure to be jealous if she missed out on any part of this. She thought of Erik and wondered how he would feel about these spur-of-the-moment plans; perhaps he'd envisioned an evening alone with her. And if they were going to be with others this evening, there would be no chance for her serious talk with Erik. "I'll call after I talk to the others," she said finally.

They pulled up in front of Calloway's Art Gallery,

double-parking as Sharon had suggested earlier. Liz handed Meg the slip of paper with the address and phone number. Brian popped the trunk and got out to collect the paintings.

Sharon appeared at the door of the gallery. "Meg," she said. "I have to talk to you."

"We'll have lots of time. Brian is dropping me off along with these; I'm going to stick around until you get off, and we'll take the subway together."

"No. I have to talk to you *now*." She pulled Meg a little aside. "Diane says that she can't take any more of your paintings for a while."

Meg stared at her friend in astonishment. "But I talked to her just last week. If she didn't want them, why didn't she call?"

"She tried, this morning, but I guess you'd already left. Anyway, I guess it would be best to leave them in Brian's trunk, if he doesn't mind." She gave a little wave to Brian as if she'd just noticed that he was there.

Meg walked back to where Brian now had four paintings stacked against the car's fender. "Put them back, if you don't mind," she said. He looked at her questioningly. "Sharon says that they're not wanted. We'll take them home with us on Sunday."

Brian shrugged, but the look that he gave Meg promised that he'd want to know more about this sudden change in plans. Sharon had once again called Meg over to where she stood at the doorway to the gallery. "There's no point in waiting around here for me, Meg," she said. "We're expecting a big shipment from uptown in just a little while. We'll all be busy unpacking, and then we'll have to decide where to hang all of it. Why don't you go on back to the apartment? Wait . . . here's my key."

Meg stared at the key in her hand. It was just as well; she didn't feel like lingering at the gallery or facing Diane Calloway right now anyway. Sharon could tell her later about the sudden change in plans. Suddenly she felt tired, grubby from the ride. "Fine, Sharon. I'll shower and take a nap." She nodded toward Brian and Liz, still standing next to the car. "Are you interested in a casual evening with Brian and Liz and their friend Jerry?"

"Sounds wonderful. I assume Julia is included? Otherwise she'd kill me if she found out."

"Yes. You, Julia, Erik, and I."

Sharon finally walked over to the car. She held out her hand. "It's good to see you again, Brian." She and Liz made little "nice to meet you" noises.

"There's a subway stop right at the corner," Meg said as she reached for her suitcase. "Thanks for everything, you two. I'm pretty certain we'll all see you tonight, but I'll call after I've confirmed with the other two." She gave a little wave and walked away, head down, hoping that none of the little group assembled by the car would notice her tears.

Chapter Nine

"**B**ut why would Diane suddenly decide that she can't show any more of your paintings? I thought that she was selling a couple every month."

Meg stared at the phone as if searching for an answer. "I don't know, Erik. Sharon said that there was a big shipment coming in. Maybe she's got a lock on somebody really hot."

"What will you do next? Will you make the rounds this afternoon?"

"No, I can't do that. The paintings are in Brian's trunk. He's in Tribeca. I suppose I could talk him into driving me around tomorrow. Anyway, right now I just want to take a shower and have a nap. I'll be at your place by eight, and we can continue down to Jerry's."

"Come on down now, Meg. It's been weeks . . ."

"I wouldn't be very good company. I'm more than

a little depressed. It was going so well, Erik, knowing that the paintings were selling, knowing that all I had to do was bring them down to Diane."

"You'll find another gallery, Meg. At least you're being productive. If you want to see 'more than a little depressed,' come on over. I seem to have written all of five pages this week. Let's see—at five pages a week, the first draft should be done in about two years."

He sounded as if he felt even worse than she did, and her heart went out in sympathy. She couldn't imagine writing a novel, just as he couldn't imagine painting a picture, but they both knew the awful feeling when inspiration refused to come. "Okay, Erik. We can cry on each other's shoulder. I'll be there soon."

She tried to decide as the water cascaded over her. Now could be a good time. She'd have the afternoon alone with Erik. She could end it now and then enjoy the evening at Jerry's without him.

Yes, she decided as she ran a comb through her wet hair. She'd tell him it was over.

She hung on to the overhead strap as the L line rattled along its subterranean path. She'd forgotten that there was never an empty seat on this line, even during the off-hours. At each station, she stared dispassionately at the graffiti scribbled on the walls. With the new slick coatings the subways were cleaner than they had been in years, but the city's young hoodlums still found ways to deface public property. She thought back to the time when she'd first arrived in the city. The scrawled obscenities had shocked her then. She'd become blind to them over the years she'd spent at

NYU, and she would not have noticed them now except that she'd become accustomed to the cleanliness of her little Vermont town.

She climbed the stairs from the subway and headed down the familiar street. Erik must have been watching at the window, because he buzzed her in almost as soon as she rang the bell. And then she was crying in his arms, surprised at her own unexpected emotions. He held her gently and stroked her long, dark hair. They talked about his disappointment with his writing, about her shock of the afternoon. Somehow Meg never did get around to telling him that she wouldn't be seeing him anymore.

Brian's friend Jerry could have been a time-traveler from the Sixties, or maybe even from nineteenth-century Paris. He was certainly the very model of the artist starving in the garret.

The first thing that Meg noticed was that there was almost no furniture. Large pillows were strewn around the living room, and, as she headed to the bathroom to check her hands and face for visible subway grime, she caught a glimpse of a mattress on the floor of the tiny bedroom.

Brian and Jerry were deep in conversation and so, after the briefest of introductions, Meg and Erik settled next to Liz near the scarred-looking coffee table that held chips and dip. Meg looked around, fascinated by this glimpse of bohemian life. Brick-and-board bookcases, filled to overflowing, lined one wall. A rather good sound system, obviously Jerry's one concession to the acquisition of material goods, produced something classical, low enough not to intrude on conversation. Large canvasses, thickly coated with paint in varying shades of off-white, covered every available wall space.

Liz caught Meg's eye and motioned toward the paintings. "Amy's," she said. "Jerry's love. She's a Bennington grad—met him when she was a student and he was there for a semester as playwright in residence. I'm surprised she's not here."

Almost on cue, the skinny blond in black tights and oversized sweater came in the door, loaded down with sacks of soft drinks. "Hi. I'm Amy," she said as she headed to the little kitchen.

She's my age, thought Meg, scarcely able to believe it. With her urchin-style hairdo, Amy looked to be about fifteen.

"Soda's in the fridge," Amy called from the kitchen. "There's plenty of ice. Help yourselves. Don't expect waitress service, because that's what I do forty hours a week." Meg thought, not for the first time, how very lucky she was. Her part-time job left her lots of time to paint and didn't leave her physically exhausted.

Amy sat down in yoga position next to Liz and Meg. The two young artists were quickly sharing their setbacks and successes with each other.

"Come on in. It's open," Jerry yelled in response to the knock on the door.

Meg studied her two oldest friends as they muttered responses to the introductions: Julia, counting heads and betraying her chagrin as she figured out that one of those females must belong to Brian. Sharon, carefully avoiding Meg's eyes. Both of them seemed just a little overdressed for a casual evening. Meg glanced again at Amy, cross-legged on the floor, and wondered how Sharon and Julia were going to accomplish that with any grace in their short, tight skirts. *My fault,* she thought. *I know Brian and Liz well enough to know they'd be in jeans. Still, if Sharon hadn't dropped that bombshell, we'd all have dressed in the apartment together and I would have had a chance to suggest what they should wear. I wouldn't have rushed down to Erik's place to cry on his shoulder.*

Julia had recovered her aplomb and sat down next to Brian and Jerry. She listened to their discussion with wide-eyed attention, nodding her head at appropriate intervals. *"Give it up,"* Meg wanted to say, but she knew that she herself was equally guilty of fantasizing about Brian, and she felt a twinge of sympathy for her friend.

Sharon skillfully folded her long legs under her as she sat down next to Erik, still avoiding Meg's eyes. There was no escape, though, because Erik plunged right in. "Meg told me that Diane doesn't want any more of her paintings. What's the story, Sharon?"

Sharon put her hand on his arm and looked at him innocently. "I was so sorry to be the one who had to break the news," she said. "We've got two new artists lined up, and we think they're really going to take off. They both do modernistic cityscapes, and so Diane has decided to use that as the gallery's theme for a while. You can see that Meg's rural scenes wouldn't fit." She turned to Meg, finally, and spread her hands in a gesture of helplessness. Then she turned back to Erik and put her hand on his arm again.

She reminds me of a slinky cat, Meg mused. *I can almost hear her purr.* The thought brought her up short, and she berated herself for the unkind thought.

Don't kill the messenger, she reminded herself. *Sharon is not to blame for the gallery's decision.*

Brian stood up and stretched, then headed to the kitchen. Julia looked around as if trying to decide how obvious she might look if she got up to follow him. He came back with two cans of soda, handing one to Liz as he sat down beside her. Julia scrunched her pillow closer to the coffee table, where Brian was expounding on Jerry's play that would be performed the next night.

And now it was Meg's friends' turn to be plied with questions. Erik sheepishly admitted what little progress he'd made on his novel, and received some real sympathy along with encouragement from Brian and Jerry. Sharon was congratulated on landing the gallery job, and Meg was pleased to search her own mind and find no trace of envy. Julia proudly announced that she was working as a sales clerk at the Museum of Modern Art's gift shop. It was perhaps not what her parents were hoping for when they'd provided over a hundred thousand dollars for her four years at NYU, but her pay covered her share of the rent on the apartment, and it allowed her to browse through her beloved MOMA every lunch hour.

Sharon and Julia had found that they could manage financially without a third roommate. "So your bed is always ready and waiting for you, Meg," Julia bubbled. "We could let Liz sleep on the sofa, too, if you two want to come down more often."

"I may take you up on that," Liz replied. "Brian usually stays here, and I bunk with Amy." She looked around as her voice trailed off, and the others laughed. A sofa would be a big step up.

* * *

Erik kissed Meg and then looked around for a cab. "Let's just roam around tomorrow, by ourselves. Maybe go down to the Seaport."

"But last night we agreed to meet Liz and Brian and Julia and the rest of the gang and roam through all the antique shops in Soho."

"I know we did, but we can cancel. We need some time together, Meg. Besides, aren't you sick to death of antique shops? That whole town you're living in is like one giant antique."

Meg felt her temper flare with his last statement. She knew that he was right, that they should just spend the day together, perhaps even talk about their relationship—or lack of same. They had to have some time alone if she was going to tell him that it was over. But his attack on Bennington brought out her stubbornness. She bit her lip. "I haven't seen Julia and Sharon in months," she began.

"You saw them last night. You'll see them again tonight," he countered. He spotted an on-duty cab and stepped toward it, hand raised.

"Good night," she said quickly. She gave him a little kiss on the cheek as he helped her into the cab and handed the driver some cash. "I'll call you tomorrow morning." As the cab pulled away she watched out the rear window. Erik walked toward the subway with his head down. His slumped shoulders showed that he knew as well as she did that their relationship was in trouble.

Meg mentally replayed the weekend during the drive back to Bennington. She was in the backseat, and she kept her eyes closed in hopes that Brian and Liz would think she was asleep. The gallery—that had been quite a blow, and yet that disappointment was overshadowed by her anger at herself for once again postponing the breakup with Erik.

She could tell that he knew that something was wrong. Maybe he wouldn't even be upset to see the end of the farce. Maybe he wanted out of the relationship just as much as she did. Why hadn't she just blurted out what she felt? Why had she leaped at any excuse to spend every minute of the weekend as part of a crowd? Now once again she'd be back in Bennington while he was in New York, and it seemed childish to end things by phone. And she didn't even know when she'd see him next.

She shifted a little and sat up to look out the window. "Penny for your thoughts," Brian said as he caught a glimpse of her in the rearview mirror.

"I was just thinking of what a great weekend it was," she lied. "Thanks for inviting me to go with you. Jerry's play is really great! We all enjoyed it."

"You'll have to come down in January while I'm there," he said.

Her heart leaped. Then she told herself that it was just a casual comment. She snuggled down into her seat and closed her eyes. *Let him think I'd like to sleep,* she said to herself. She turned her thoughts once again back to Erik, berating herself for her hesitation to put an end to whatever it was that they had once thought they shared.

The snow began as they neared the Vermont border. Meg roused herself from her reverie as she tuned in to Brian's comment. "That's it, ladies. You won't see bare ground again until April."

"I'll come and visit you, Brian," Liz purred, putting her hand on his arm. "They keep the sidewalks shoveled in the city."

The city. It hadn't sunk in when Brian had talked about it just a little while ago, but now Meg remembered that he would be in New York for the last half of December and all of January. She would have no teaching duties. She could spend the Christmas holidays and all of January in New York if she wanted to. Sharon and Julia would probably appreciate the chance to divide six weeks of rent by three instead of by two. She could see Erik, could tell him that she'd decided that they had no future together. She relaxed, gazing at the heavily falling snow until she drifted off to sleep.

Brian helped her carry her rejected paintings back to the sunporch. Brandy nearly knocked her over in her excitement. Fang hung back, pretending to be offended at being fed by a student a mere twice a day during Meg's absence. "Would you and Liz like coffee, Brian?" she asked.

He looked out at the snow. "Better not. It's still coming down hard. I'd better get Liz on home, and then collect Michael and get home myself. Do you need anything? I should have stopped in town so we could load up on milk and bread."

"Thanks anyway, Brian. I have a full freezer, a good supply of pet food, and I drink my coffee black. It can snow three feet for all I care."

"Bite your tongue! We never cancel classes. I know that you can walk over from here if you can't get your car out of your driveway, but tromping through three feet of cold, wet, white stuff could be a real challenge."

Meg waved good-bye. The snow was falling faster now. She could see the swirling flakes in the gathering twilight. She turned on most of the lights in the downstairs rooms and pushed the thermostat up a notch.

Fang wrapped himself around her leg and mewed plaintively. "Starved, are you?" she asked as she headed to the kitchen. She scooped an extra measure of food into each bowl. "What would you do if I were gone for six weeks?" She repeated it to herself, in a whisper, as if only just realizing what she'd said. Six weeks. Yes, she could find one of the few students who would be staying in town and working locally during the January term. Liz, in fact, had mentioned hiring one to work in the gallery, perhaps, Meg realized with sudden insight, so that she could more easily trek down to New York. It wouldn't be hard to find someone to care for Brandy and Fang. Perhaps Liz's student helper would even like to live here, in the house, since the dorms would be closed until February.

Meg brewed herself a pot of coffee and struck a match to the already laid logs and kindling in the fireplace. She curled up on the couch. Brandy flopped down in front of the fire, and Fang made herself comfortable on Meg's lap. Meg absentmindedly stroked the little cat. *Six weeks,* she thought. *No, that's impossible. I have responsibilities here. Two weeks, maybe,*

When the phone rang she assumed it was Erik, but

the "Meggie?" told her immediately that it was her brother. "Meggie? Want to spend Christmas with us?"

Well, if she couldn't go to New York she couldn't go to Boston either. "I think I'll just stay here, John," she said. "I've got the cat and the dog. This is home. I think I'd like to be home for the holidays."

"It might not be too cheery, Meggie. Last Christmas we were all there together. It won't be the same without Mom and Dad."

"It's not the same every day without Mom and Dad. I *live* here, remember? Sooner or later I'll have to face a Christmas in my own home without them. It might as well be now. For that matter, you might as well face it now, too. Why don't you and Pam and the kids come here?" For just a moment Meg imagined the big tree in the parlor, remembered her niece and nephew rushing down the stairs on Christmas morning. . . .

"It makes no sense, Meggie. We always came *because* of Mom and Dad. Not that we don't want to see you, but it's time for us to build our own traditions in our own house. And you can be part of that."

"Thanks, John. Maybe it's time for me to build my traditions in my own, house, too. I appreciate the offer, though. I'll come to see you soon, I promise."

She hung up the phone feeling more alone than she'd ever felt. She stared out at the accumulating snow. She picked up the little cat and nuzzled it against her neck as she talked to it absentmindedly. "I think we're on our own," she said. "Brian will be in New York. Liz will be visiting Brian. And we'll be here, the three of us."

Chapter Ten

Brian stomped the snow off his boots in the entranceway and then dragged the big tree through the double doors of the sunporch and into the parlor. Michael followed him, stomping his boots in imitation of his father. Liz brought up the rear. "We're going to have to cut at least eight inches off the bottom," Brian said.

Meg felt a bit sheepish about the size of the tree; she'd looked up at it where it grew and argued with Brian that it wasn't—couldn't possibly be—more than nine feet tall, but once they had cut it down it was clear even to her that ten feet would have been a better guess. "I'll use the branches to make a wreath," she said defensively.

"You can use the extra branches to make several wreaths," he countered. "I'll take them to New York with me if you like. I have a friend who owns a small gift shop in Soho. The yuppies will buy them. You can't sell them here—everyone makes their own."

His comments reminded Meg all too forcefully that he would be leaving in just a few days. The semester was drawing to a close. Their expedition to cut the tree, followed by dinner and tree-trimming at Meg's house, was to be the last time she and Brian and Michael and Liz would be together until February. Meg looked over Brian's shoulder at Liz, who didn't seem to share her concern. Well, Liz had plans to spend Christmas in New York.

I could have done that too, Meg thought. *I could have hired Kenny from next door to feed Brandy and Fang, and trekked off to the city. By next week I could have been looking at the Metropolitan Museum's fifty-foot tree. I could have been listening to medieval carols at the Cloisters.*

She gazed up at the tree, now shorter and secure in its stand, its top nearly brushing the ceiling. A lump formed in her throat as she recognized how important this ritual was to her, how badly she needed to celebrate the holiday here, even if Brandy and Fang were her only company.

She had brought the boxes of ornaments down from the attic the day before, and now she retrieved them from the stairway and put them on a small table near the tree. "The ladder's still in the basement, Brian," she said. "I tried to bring it upstairs, but it was a little too heavy for me."

He headed for the basement, followed by Liz. Meg started after them, and then stopped. It would be an easy enough job for two, and a third person would only be in the way. She walked back to the stairs and retrieved the boxes of tree lights.

"Play the piano," Brian shouted from the basement entrance. "This job calls for Christmas music."

Brian and Liz started putting on the lights. Meg covered her feelings by leafing through her big book of Christmas music. She played "Silent Night" and then looked for something especially for Michael, maybe reindeer and elves. She settled for "Here Comes Santa Claus." Everybody sang along, with Michael trying his best to imitate the adults. "Rudolf" was followed by "Jingle Bells" and then by "Frosty the Snowman." Finally Meg hit a resounding chord which announced the end of the recital.

She turned on the radio so that the music could continue while she headed to the kitchen to put a casserole in the oven. She warmed the cider and returned to the living room carrying a tray with three steaming mugs and one slightly cooler one, a cinnamon stick protruding from each. "Heavenly," Liz said, sniffing appreciatively as she reached for a mug.

Liz balanced the ladder while Brian stood on it to put the star on the top of the tree. Meg helped Michael hang some unbreakable ornaments on the tree's lower branches. Fang batted one off and chased it across the floor. Michael picked it up and hung it back on the tree. Fang batted it again as everybody laughed at this new game.

After supper Michael fell asleep on the rug in front of the fire with Brandy curled up against him. The adults again sang along with the radio's music. The ever-present snow accumulated silently outside the windows, adding to the holiday atmosphere. Meg felt her depression lift. Her parents were gone, but she had new friends and, she thought as she watched Fang batting a wayward Christmas ball, a new little family.

Several more inches of snow had fallen during the night. As Brian had predicted, Meg left her car in the garage and walked along the dirt road and through the meadow to the college. Her old ski pants, rescued from a trunk in the attic, kept her warm and dry. She decided that she might never have to shovel the driveway, then amended that thought as she realized that she would eventually run out of pet food. On her next trip to the grocery store, she vowed, she'd buy enough to last the rest of the winter.

Two more days of classes, then Brian would be gone. Meg was finally gaining some perspective on Brian as she learned to think of him more as a big brother and less as a prospective love. Brian belonged to Liz.

Meg had come to rely on Brian in many ways, and she would miss him dreadfully for the next six weeks, but she told herself that she would miss him as a *friend,* just as she would miss Liz when she was in New York.

The storm struck as if it had been waiting for classes to end. Meg congratulated herself, she had shoveled the driveway and made her grocery store trek just before the snow started in earnest. She had brought fireplace wood inside and stacked it in the pantry. Now she brought a few logs into the living room and was soon settled down in front of a roaring fire, dog at her feet, cat on her lap, and a cup of hot chocolate on the table at her elbow.

By the next morning, the bare branches of the oak trees were covered in ice. Icicles hung from the eaves. Brandy hesitated, and then ran out and rolled in the snow. Fang opted for his indoor litter box. Meg gathered up her camera and a fresh canvas and charcoal for sketching, hoping to capture the pristine whiteness. She layered on jeans and ski pants, sweatshirt and ski jacket, and topped it all off with knitted cap, scarf, and gloves. She trudged through the meadow with the dog gamboling behind her, then took the path off to the right towards the river.

Perfect, she thought. Little eddies of water made their way through the snow and ice, glinting in the morning sunlight, with the water looking every bit as frigid as Meg knew it must be. The trees bent low over the riverbank, waiting to drop the snow from their loaded branches with the first warming of the sun. The rough surface of the cobblestones of the old mill provided a striking contrast to the water and ice. Meg would sketch it quickly now, before her fingers grew too numb to move. She took some photographs so that she could see the scene later, when she was actually ready to paint. Unlike her wildflowers, the snow scene would not be painted on the spot with Meg lying on her belly. She shivered at the thought.

Another brief stop on the way back to the house produced a sketch of snow drifted up against a stone wall. Meg knew that these paintings would be difficult to do well; so much white required nuances of shading that she'd not yet tried. This new season excited her and left her eager to master the necessary techniques.

She wished that Amy, who did those marvelous all-white canvasses, were here to help her with her first efforts of white-on-white.

At home and warm again, she painted nonstop for the rest of the day. She was reminded of the time as the small kitten wound itself around her legs and me-owed softly. Meg stepped back to look at the painting of the mill and the river, and nodded approvingly to herself. It was good. It was at least as good as the wildflowers. Yes, she thought as she headed to the kitchen to open a can of catfood, she would enjoy the winter.

Snow pictures accumulated almost as rapidly as the snow itself. Meg could now look out her first-floor windows and see the snow just a few inches below the sill. Brandy seemed to have tapped into some ancestral memory of carrying kegs of Couvoisier to travelers stranded in the Alps, because she continued to enjoy her daily romps in the deep snow. Meg had not seen so much snow since she was a small child. Television reports confirmed that impression. The storm was being referred to as the blizzard of the decade.

On Christmas Eve Meg stood at the front door and sketched, trying to capture the fury of the latest onslaught. Sleet lashed against the windows and formed a new layer of ice over the tree limbs. She wondered if she could convey the power of this storm, or whether her painting would look as peaceful as a Christmas card.

She put another log on the fire and settled down with Brandy and Fang. The Christmas tree stood in the corner of the room, right where it had been for as many Christmases as Meg could remember. The radio played all the old, familiar carols.

The phone rang, and Fang leaped up in surprise and ran into the kitchen. "Merry Christmas, Meg," the familiar voice said.

"And to you too, Erik," she replied.

"Are you okay? The television reports make your storm look pretty wicked."

"I think we've got about three feet on the ground. It's supposed to stop sometime tonight, though. Listen—my radio station's playing 'I'm Dreaming of a White Christmas.' I suspect most people here are dreaming of Florida, but I'm actually enjoying it. And you should see Brandy—she loves the snow."

"You're not too lonely?"

"I'm lonely, but not too lonely."

"What about New Year's weekend? I could come up then, Meg."

She hesitated. She was certain that things with Erik were really over, even though once in a while she pretended that there was a relationship to save. Still, they had to talk, and it would be easier here than in New York. "That would be nice, Erik," she said finally. "I'll book you a room at Grandma's House again."

"It would really make more sense for me to stay at your house."

They'd had this argument before, back in the fall. They argued a little, but Meg again stood her ground. She said good-bye to Erik and then dialed Grandma's House, where she was pleased to find that there was a single available for New Year's weekend. She settled back in with the cat on her lap and the dog at her feet.

On Christmas Day, Meg decided to shovel out her driveway. Brandy "helped," as expected, as she rolled in snowdrifts and raced back and forth between the garage and the house. Fang watched them from the sunporch with a tilt of the head which seemed to say that he was the smart one, indoors and warm.

When the driveway was clear, Meg decided that she might as well go for a drive. As usual, she loaded up her camera and sketch pads and charcoal just in case she stumbled on a scene that called out to be painted. She whistled for Brandy, who leaped in the car beside her. She waved at Fang and headed toward the mountains.

The roads had been plowed and salted and were far more passable than Meg had thought they might be. She drove to the overlook that was such a favorite with the tourists, where she spent an hour trying to capture the white-capped peaks against the gray sky. The air felt heavy, as if the snow were just waiting to fall, but it was good to be outside after a couple of days when she'd not ventured further than her own back door.

The phone was ringing as she opened the back door. She pulled off her boots in the pantry and padded across the kitchen in her stocking feet. Her brother's cheery voice caused a twinge of loneliness—she could have been with him and his family, celebrating Christmas together. The children excitedly told her everything that Santa had brought, and she thought about what fun it would have been to watch them as they opened their presents. Well, it had been her choice. She assured Pam and John that she was fine, that she was enjoying this quiet Christmas Day, and that Erik would be up to visit the next weekend. No, she told them, she had not cooked a turkey, but she did have a Cornish hen and had actually made a pie. She told them about her trip with Brian and Liz and Michael to cut the tree, and all about the fun that they'd had decorating it. "It's far too big, of course," she said, "but I couldn't resist. I'll be sorry when it comes time to take it down. I'll be on my own for that. Of course it could come down while Erik's here, but I really wanted to have it up for the week after New Years's."

She was stoking the fire when the phone rang again. "Merry Christmas again," Erik said.

"I didn't expect to hear from you again today." She remembered that his parents would be in New York for the holiday weekend. They'd planned to see the ice-skaters at Rockefeller Center and the Christmas tree at the Metropolitan Museum and all the rest of the touristy things. "How are your parents? Did you get to Rockefeller Center?"

"Yes. One thing crossed off the list." He hesitated. "Listen, Meg. I've got a problem. The folks have decided to stay all week."

"Oh." There didn't seem to be anything to say. She waited.

"It really has been quite a while since they've spent much time here," he said apologetically. "Dad just decided to call in to work tomorrow and tell them that he's taking three more vacation days. They won't be leaving until the day after New Year's."

Meg swallowed hard. "I understand, Erik," she said, missing her own parents more than ever. They made small talk for a little while, and then she wished him a Merry Christmas and said good-night.

Meg called Grandma's House to cancel Erik's

room. *Maybe it's for the best*, she thought. *It would be a little unfair to have him make the trip here only to learn that it's over. Better in New York, in his own apartment, where I can just leave and go back to Sharon and Julia's after our talk. But I'm not sure I want to be there for two weeks. One week will be more than enough.*

Meg sat and stroked the little cat. Liz was in New York with Brian; school was closed until February. Meg almost wished that she'd gone to Boston to spend the holiday with John and Pam.

Fang jumped down and ran to the window to investigate as a mound of snow fell from a tree branch outside. Meg got up and put another log on the fire.

On the day after Christmas, Meg decided that she had better make the best of the life she'd chosen. She walked into town, enjoying the crisp, cold air. It was pleasant to browse through the gift shops, looking at pottery and crystal and jewelry. She drove to the little cluster of antique shops on the outskirts of town, where she enjoyed looking even as she forced herself to resist buying furniture that she didn't need. Finally she drove back into town and parked in front of Liz's gallery. She'd wondered what student was minding the store and was pleased to find that it was Sally, whom she knew from one of her classes.

"Hi, Sally," she said. "I wondered who was taking over for Liz."

"Hi, Ms. Ryan," the bubbly blond replied. "Yes, I'm the lucky one. This is such a super fieldwork job for me. Ms. Roberts says that I can continue part time, on Saturdays, after the next term starts, too. She'll let me help with the bookkeeping and the ordering. I want to have a gallery like this after I graduate, so I want to learn all I can."

"Are you local, Sally? Where are you staying?"

"My parents live just about an hour away, Ms. Ryan, so I'm staying with them for the January term . . . you know, the dorms are closed. I don't mind the drive, though the roads have been icy some mornings. Anyway, for the next two weeks I'm staying right here! Ms. Roberts is in New York City, and she said she'd be just as happy to have someone staying in the apartment. You know she lives just above the shop. What could be more convenient! I don't even care how much it snows."

"I can't offer a deal like that," Meg said, "but I can offer you a place in town for the third week of January. That's when *I'll* be in New York, and I need someone to stay in my house and take care of my dog and cat. Are you interested?"

"Golly, yes, Ms. Ryan. That would be super."

"Are there other students in town?" Meg asked. "You must be lonely here by yourself."

"It seems really wonderful to have a place to be by myself, Ms. Ryan. I've got two younger sisters at home, so sometimes I feel as if I never have a minute's privacy. And the dorm . . ."

"I remember," Meg said, making a little face.

"Actually," Sally said as she returned to the question, "there are—let me see—five of us in town or nearby this January." She ticked off names on her fingers. "Valerie is working at set production at the Williamstown Theater. Connie—her family has money so she can afford to volunteer—is cataloging materials at the Williamstown museum. Ruth is on a research project at Sterling-Winthrop, doing some biology thing I don't really understand. Rachel is working at Annie's Antiques here in town. At least a few of us get together almost every night, sometimes for dinner, sometimes for a movie." She thought for a minute. "You're alone, too, aren't you? I know that you mostly hang out with Professor Davidson and Ms. Roberts, and they're both in the city."

"Yes," Meg said. "I'm beginning to realize that I should have spent the fall term meeting more people. I'd forgotten about the January exodus."

"Would you like to come with us tonight?" Sally asked hesitantly. "I'm driving over to Williamstown to meet Valerie and Connie. We're eating Chinese, and then going to see the Williams-Amherst hockey game. But maybe that seems too college-kid to you?"

"I was a college kid only last year, Sally. Yes, I'd love to come. But only if you can learn to call me Meg instead of Ms. Ryan. I could drive, if you like. Maybe you'd like to come to my house when the shop closes, so you can see what you've volunteered for."

Meg drove home feeling cheery again. She needed some new friends, and this little group of Bennington women would be a good start.

Chapter Eleven

"I'd like to come down for the third week of January," Meg said. "I'll pay my share of the rent."

"Gee, Meg, that sounds great. Wait till I tell Sharon." Julia sounded really excited about Meg's plans. "Of course, we'll be working all day . . ."

"That's okay, Julia. I can certainly amuse myself in New York. I have lots of shopping to do, and I'm having withdrawal symptoms because it's been so long since I've been to the Metropolitan Museum. When Erik said that his parents planned to visit, to see that wonderful tree with its Neapolitan angels, I was green with envy. Of course the tree will be down by the time I'm there, but I could spend a whole day in the Egyptian wing and not care if I saw anything else."

"I can get you a pass for MOMA," Julia said. "And you can meet me there at noon any day you want. I'm always ready to give up my lunch hour to spend it in the museum. Yogurt at my desk is a small penalty to pay."

"That sounds great, Julia. I'll see you in two weeks, then."

Meg hung up the phone and poured herself a cup of coffee. She sat at the kitchen table, enjoying the sunlight pouring in, and reflected on the past six months. She could be living in New York, sharing an apartment with her old friends. Maybe she'd still be going out with Erik. She would be wearing chic little black dresses and selling paintings at a popular gallery. Instead, she was planning to end things with Erik. She was living alone in this huge house in the middle of nowhere, sharing her life with her dog and her cat, helping with the art classes at the college, and doing more painting—and better, she told herself—than she had ever done before. She had a new group of friends, Brian and Liz and now Sally and the other Bennington women. Her life had been heading in a certain direction when suddenly she had taken a branch off the main road.

Talking to Julia about the Metropolitan's great tree reminded her that it was time to confront a job she'd been postponing. She got up and climbed the stairs to the attic and brought down the empty boxes that would hold the Christmas ornaments. She put on a CD of carols; it seemed like appropriate music for the end of the season. She packed each ornament carefully in its own little niche. She balanced on the ladder to reach the lights near the top of the tree. Finally the huge tree was bare. She used her turkey baster to slurp the water out of the tree stand and into a bucket. She put on her dad's old work gloves and reached through the branches to grab the thick trunk. She slowly tipped it toward her, catching it with both hands before it hit the floor. She dragged it through the kitchen and out the back door. She rested a minute, then pulled it out to the wild area far behind the garage. The birds might enjoy it as a winter refuge.

She was exhausted by the time she sat down with a cup of tea, but she felt proud. She'd had plenty of help in putting the tree up. She thought that Erik would be there to help take it down. But the difficult task was finished, and she'd accomplished it by herself. She was becoming more and more self-sufficient as the months went by, months of learning to live alone.

The snow came down with a fury that showed Meg that the Christmas storm had been only a dress rehearsal. As the accumulation continued and the travel warnings began, she was thankful that she'd stocked up on pet food and kitty litter.

"Good thing it's January term," she said to the cat next morning when she looked out and saw that the snow reached the windowsill. "I'll shovel a path so Brandy can get out for a run. Then we'll build another fire."

Her cheeks stung by the time she finished. The snow had turned to sleet, and it showed no signs of stopping. The radio spluttered static. She tried another station with the same result.

She put on a CD, unwilling to face the silence. Brahms comforted her as she laid the fire. She put the coffeepot on and dropped a piece of bread in the toaster. The toast popped up just as the music stopped. She hadn't really been listening, but it didn't seem as if the sonata had ended. She realized that the coffeepot was no longer gurgling. She tried a light switch. Nothing.

Surely the electricity will be back on soon, she told herself. But, as she looked out the front window and saw the ice buildup on the power lines, she knew that she was indulging in wishful thinking.

She lit one of the candles on the dining room table and carried it up the stairs to the attic. She thought she remembered seeing . . . ah, there it was. An oil lamp, still half filled. She carried it down to the kitchen. The power might come back on soon, but she'd better be prepared.

Let's see, she said to herself as she munched on the now-cold toast. *Can opener.* She rummaged in a drawer until she found one that didn't need to be plugged in. *More candles.* The old stove was gas, so she could boil water for tea. Or instant coffee, if she got desperate enough.

She filled the bathtub with water. She didn't know why, but some long-ago memory told her that it should be done. Downstairs, she filled the kitchen sink also. As an afterthought, she brought in a bucket from the laundry and filled that as well.

She was congratulating herself on her fine preparations when she realized that the kitchen was chilly. She checked to see that she'd shut the back door tightly after shoveling the path for Brandy. She put her hand on the radiator—nearly stone cold. She realized that the thermostat had an electric switch. She knew that the big reservoir had been filled with fuel oil just a few days before, but the ancient boiler would not get the signal to heat the house.

Her shoulders sagged. The drafty old house would cool down quickly. She put her ski suit on again. The "Brandy path" would have to be extended to the garage, where her winter supply of firewood was stacked. She squared her shoulders and grabbed the shovel.

Two hours later her hands were blistered and her arms ached. Only Brandy seemed to enjoy the outdoor activity, happy for the unexpected company. Meg longed for nothing more than a hot shower, but she was too tired to climb the stairs to the chilly bathroom. She settled for a chair in front of the blazing fire, with the two animals nestled at her feet.

Meg awoke to find the fire dying. She put on another log and tossed in some newspaper. She poked at the hot coals until she managed to get the fire going again. She glanced at her watch. She'd slept for hours!

It was already dark, though it was only late afternoon. She lit the candle and walked out into the frigid kitchen. She fed the animals and opened a can of soup for herself. While she waited for it to heat, she picked up the phone to call Liz. Dead. She should have known.

She carried the candle and the soup back into the living room by the fire. She had never felt so alone, so cut off from human companionship. She missed her parents more than ever before. She resented their deaths. They'd left her alone when she needed them.

She finished her soup and boiled some water for tea.

While the tea steeped she climbed the stairs to her bedroom to get pillows and blankets. She'd bring them down by the fire so that she could sleep in front of the fireplace that night. She was certain that Brandy and Fang would cuddle as close to her as they could get.

This was the time, she realized as she sipped her tea, when her New York friends had predicted she'd tire of Vermont. This was the time of testing, a time to discover if her love of Bennington was real enough to sustain her. This was the time to summon her own inner resources—to decide whether she would stay here permanently or whether she would give up.

The first challenge came next morning. Meg turned on the tap to fill the kettle, and nothing came out. It took her a few minutes to realize that the pipes must be frozen. Now she knew why she had filled the sink and the bathtub. The sink would provide water for coffee or tea, and a bucketful of water from the tub could be dumped in the toilet to make it flush. Meg was proud of her ability to cope with this storm. The problems she faced now made taking down a Christmas tree seem like child's play. She did wish, though, that she'd taken that hot shower the day before.

For the next two days, Meg painted by oil lamp in front of the fire. When she tired of painting, she snuggled into her self-made nest with the animals at her feet. She kept the "Brandy path" clear as she trekked to the garage several times a day for another load of wood.

On the third day she heard the snowplow. Even as she ran to the window to look, the kitchen light came on. She heard the old furnace rumble to a start. *Maybe the phone's back too*, she thought, but that was not to be.

Meg climbed the stairs to her still-frigid bedroom. She shed her clothes, put on her woolly bathrobe and slippers, and headed for the hot shower she'd been dreaming of.

The house warmed up quickly. Meg was just settling back in front of the fire when she heard a strange sound from the kitchen. Water running! Had she left the tap turned on when she'd learned that she had no water?

She walked into the kitchen to greet the latest disaster. Water gushed from the cabinet beneath her kitchen sink. She slipped across the wet floor and opened the cabinet. A fountain spurted from a broken pipe. She remembered, belatedly, that her father used to leave the water running a little in the kitchen during the freezing weather. The old pipes here were too close to the outside of the poorly-insulated house. When the water inside froze and expanded, the pressure was too much for the old plumbing to withstand.

She tried to remember where the main shut-off valve was. Basement, she thought. She ran down the stairs, frantically looking around. She spotted the object of her search and breathed a sigh of relief. But when she tried to turn the valve, it refused to move.

She reached for a wrench, happy that her father's tools were so well organized on the pegboard on the wall. She clamped the wrench onto the rusty valve and pushed on the handle. The old valve broke off at the stem.

Meg stared at the new fountain of water. Her mind raced. There was another cut-off valve, she thought. Outside, right at the front corner of the house. Buried, no doubt, under four feet of snow. She ran back upstairs and grabbed the shovel, sparing just a moment to glance at the water cascading over the kitchen floor.

An hour later the shut-off valve had been uncovered and turned off and most of the water had been mopped up from the downstairs of the house. The basement was flooded. She put on her highest boots and went down to make sure that nothing of value was on the floor, soaked with water.

She wanted to collapse, but she forced herself to check the phone book for the nearest plumber. She picked up the phone. Nothing. She'd forgotten.

By the next day the phones were back. The plumber was first on her list. "You're about tenth in line, lady," he said. "Might not be until tomorrow."

She choked back tears. "Whenever you can get here," she said politely. She gave him the address.

"You're Meggie Ryan?" he asked as he recognized the house number. "You're there by yourself, aren't you?" She nodded, not even aware that he couldn't see her. "I'll put you at the top of my list, honey. Half an hour, Meggie."

While she waited for the plumber there were calls from Erik, from John, from Julia, from Brian. She assured each of them that she was fine. Later, she thought, she'd tell them about the electricity and the burst pipe.

"Basement flooded?" the big man asked after replacing all of the plumbing under the sink.

"How did you know?" *At least this section of pipe*

won't burst again, she told herself. *Other sections of the old plumbing, maybe, but not this piece.*

"I could see where you shoveled to uncover the outside shut-off. Couldn't have been easy. All that water was still gushing out of this pipe. Had to go somewhere. Didn't know that there is always a shut-off valve in the basement, below the frost line, eh?"

There was still that mess to deal with. "I found it," she said. "It broke off. I haven't even thought of cleaning up the basement."

"Got a sump pump, don't you?"

"A what?" Just when she thought she'd learned everything about this old house—like letting the faucet drip during freezing weather—there was something new.

"Sump," he said as he headed to the basement. "Thought your father bought a sump pump when we had that wet spring a few years back."

She put on her boots and followed him down the stairs. "Here," he said. He flipped a switch.

The pump gurgled reassuringly. Meg watched as the water level receded. "You'll still have some cleaning up to do," he said, "but you won't need to stand in six inches of water while you're doing it."

Meg and Liz finally talked that evening. "I camped out at the high school," Liz said. "That's the designated shelter in this area. I guess I thought you knew. They have a generator, and, since school was canceled, there was plenty of that yummy cafeteria food on hand. Hot showers, too, in the locker rooms."

"I envy you the showers. That was the one thing missing here."

"The *one* thing? You had no heat and no electricity. You had nothing, really. I worried about you. I tried to call, to tell you about the high school, but of course the phones were down."

"I had an oil lamp. I had the fireplace, and lots of wood. I had Brandy and Fang."

Chapter Twelve

Meg put the finishing touches on the painting she'd begun during the storm. The sky in the picture looked heavy, just as it had before the snow began to fall. Meg stepped back, pleased at how she had captured that sense of impending snow. She looked around the sunporch at the others she'd done since the college semester had ended—five large paintings in addition to the one on the easel, all snow and ice and storm and winter. *They're good*, she thought. *Diane will like them.*

She'd take all of them with her, Meg decided. She'd let Diane see them first, but Calloway's was not the only gallery in New York. Living alone during this harsh winter had taught Meg how to be more self-sufficient, how to recognize what needed to be done, and how to take charge of her own life. Six months ago . . . even two months ago . . . she wasn't ready to

116

drag her paintings from dealer to dealer in a search to find someone who wanted them. Just a short time ago she had no friends in Bennington except for Liz and Brian. Meg felt as if she'd passed a test. It was the middle of January. She'd weathered the storm and proved that she could cope with whatever crises came her way. It would not be long until school began again, not long until Brian and Michael would be back in town. The winter was perhaps half over. Spring would come, and the wildflowers would burst into bloom.

Liz was back in town now. Meg was meeting her for dinner. In an outstanding case of bad timing, Liz had arrived back from her first stay in New York just in time for the big blizzard. By the time the roads were clear, she'd been more than ready to escape to the city for another week. But now she was back, and Meg was eager to hear about her most recent New York trek.

"So," Meg began, "tell me everything. How is Brian? How is the play progressing? What shows did you see? Did you buy anything special?"

"Wait," Liz protested, "I can't keep up with you. One question at a time. Let's start with Brian. Something very interesting has happened. Jerry's play is still on; it's moved to a larger space, off-Broadway but in a really hot area. He's actually making some money! People are beginning to talk options. But listen! Here's the big news! A few days ago Tony, who has the lead, was in an accident—I mean a bad accident, like he'll be out for months. Brian took over the part, and he's already had some great reviews. So he won't be back in January. He's already talked to his dean and has arranged to be on leave for the spring semester. So he's actually making money too. Of course his own play is on hold. There's no time to write. But there will be plenty of time when Tony comes back, or when Jerry's play runs its course."

"Wow," Meg said, overwhelmed by the news. She was thrilled for Jerry and Brian, of course, but she would really miss Brian and Michael when school started in February. She'd been looking forward to lunch with Brian in the Commons, to cooking dinner for him and Liz and Michael, to having him to lean on when she needed him.

"What arrangements has he made for Michael?" Meg asked.

"He's put him in the nursery school two mornings a week; he was to start in the fall anyway, so he's ready. Michael's been talking about school for months. And Brian has really been lucky. The Bennington students who are in New York for fieldwork term have really adopted the kid. They take turns staying at Jerry's apartment during the evenings. In the daytime, when Michael's not at nursery school, the students share the duties of sledding in Central Park, building snowmen . . . that child has never had so much attention. By February, when the fieldwork students are back here, Michael should be ready to adapt to every-day nursery. It will still mean a baby-sitter most nights, but Mike will be pretty tuckered out after his long day. He'll be ready for bed just about when Brian and Jerry leave for the theater, so Brian's not feeling too guilty. I assured him that single mothers manage schedules like this all the time."

"I'm going to New York next Friday," Meg said.

"I'll be in the city for a week. Maybe I can help too, during the day when all my friends are at work."

Liz raised an eyebrow. "If baby-sitting is your favorite New York City activity," she said, making it clear that it hadn't been hers. "I saw a couple of your friends," Liz added. Meg had been only half listening, still absorbing the news that Brian wouldn't be back until . . . when? Summer? Next fall? "I was at the ballet and ran into Erik and the blond . . . Sharon?"

"Sharon and Erik were at the ballet?" Meg's voice and face showed her surprise, and Liz looked chagrined.

"I thought you all hung around together," Liz said, trying to undo her words.

"Not really," Meg said. "Once in a while Erik and I went to a concert or a play with Sharon and her date, or Julia and her date. But Erik doesn't really know Sharon and Julia all that well. I mean, he knows them because they were college friends of mine, but we were never all part of the same gang. Erik and I spent more time with his fraternity brothers and their dates than we ever did with Sharon and Julia."

"Maybe Julia and Sharon had tickets and then Julia couldn't go." Liz was grasping at straws now, and they both knew it.

Meg thought back to the evening at Jerry's, when Sharon seemed to be snuggling up to Erik. "And maybe Sharon *claimed* that she and Julia had tickets but that Julia couldn't go. Even I know that ploy. But why Erik? He's mine," she said, and then wondered what made her make that ridiculous claim.

Liz put her hand over Meg's. "He *was* yours, Meg.

You left him behind. He'd seem like fair game to me, if I were Sharon. You didn't mind when she got the job you didn't want. Perhaps she thinks that you won't mind if she gets the man you don't want, also."

Meg bit her lip, but Liz didn't recognize that as the "I don't want to listen to this" signal. "I'm not so sure that Erik is the right man for you," Liz continued. "You seem comfortable with him, but not madly in love. Maybe you need to meet some new men. Perhaps Brian will have some ideas, when he gets back in town."

"I'm sorry, Meg," Julia said over the phone. "A couple of old friends of Sharon's are coming to town almost exactly for the dates that I told you were okay. Sharon already told them that they could bunk here. They've already got their plane tickets and everything."

"I could sleep on the couch."

"Gee, Meg, I don't really think this place is big enough for five. One person will *already* be on the couch. And there's only one bathroom, remember. We'll probably be tripping over each other as it is, with four."

Meg hung up and paced the floor. Sharon and Erik at the ballet. Sharon's friends arriving for the two weeks at the end of January. Someone didn't want her in New York. Sharon? Or Erik? Or both.

She called Liz and described the situation. "Go anyway," Liz said. "I'll call Jerry and see if you can stay with Amy."

"I really *have* to go," Meg said. "I'd decided to take some paintings down and search for a new gallery. Of course I could do that later, when Sharon and Julia's spare bed *is* available, but I have everything lined up for that week. Yes, Liz, please call Jerry."

The days that followed were bitterly cold. Meg began to question the wisdom of staying in Bennington. She gave some thought to looking for a job in New York, and then wondered what she would do with a Saint Bernard who loved rolling in the snow. Brian had said that he'd take Brandy if she ever decided to leave, but she was certain she couldn't just give up her furry friend. And, of course, she hadn't even been trying to sell the house, and she was under contract at the college until the end of May. She reminded herself again that the winter was half over, and that she had to expect the first winter to be the hardest. It was funny to think back to her high school days, when this weather seemed perfectly normal. It never ceased to amaze her that she could drive three hours south to New York and escape most of the fierce storms that hovered over these mountains.

She was lonely in a way that she'd not been before. She spent many evenings with Liz or with Sally and her friends, but she realized that she hadn't built the kind of close relationships that she had with Julia and Sharon . . . or that she'd thought she had, she amended.

Amy had been thrilled at the idea of a house guest who was volunteering to pay half the rent for a week. "It's just a studio," she said over the phone when she called to issue the invitation, "but the couch is pretty comfortable. I've had overnight visitors before, and nobody has complained too much."

Calling Erik had taken some courage. Meg wondered what Sharon might have told him. Finally she decided to stick to the bare facts. "I'm not staying with Sharon and Julia this trip," she explained. "I'll be at Amy's—you remember, Jerry's friend. I'm going to be scouting for a new gallery, so it will be really convenient to be in the Village."

"Call me when you get to town," he said. "Want to see a show on your first night? Or will you be tired from the drive? We could just go out to dinner and then watch TV if you'd rather."

She took the easy way out. "A show would be great, Erik. The drive won't be too bad unless we have another blizzard. I've been feeling a little house-bound, so I'll be eager to get out and do things." *And less than eager to tell you that our relationship is over*, she said to herself.

Meg finished one more painting and began to wrap them for the trip. She had shown Sally the routine that the cat and dog were accustomed to, gave her directions for the dishwasher and the washing machine, and assured her that it was all right to keep the heat set at whatever temperature she found comfortable. She made up the bed in the best guest room and laid in a huge supply of pet food so that Sally wouldn't have to shop for Brandy and Fang.

Meg perused her closet, trying to come up with a week of city clothes. One little black dress, two wool skirts . . . she could get by. She didn't really want to spend her time shopping for things she'd never wear in Bennington. At least she had her dressy boots, some good-looking flats for museum days, and one nice pair of heels for evening. Her black cape had not been worn since her parents' funeral; when she was in the city last the weather had still been pleasant enough for her soft gray leather coat. Since the appropriate attire for Bennington was the ubiquitous ski jacket, the black cape would probably never wear out; ten years from now she'd still be wearing it whenever she made a winter trip to New York.

Fang persisted in crawling into the suitcase, burrowing under the steadily accumulating pile of clothes. Meg wondered for the tenth time what her chances were of finding a new gallery. Still, the trip would be worthwhile—she would talk to Erik and close that chapter of her life.

She picked up the phone and called Amy. "Can I come a couple of days early?" she asked. "I'm all packed and ready, and sitting here watching the snow doesn't seem like a productive way to spend my time." When the answer was in the affirmative, she said, "I'll just have to call my house-sitter and see if it's all right with her. If I can reach her, I'll call you back again right away. If not, I'll let you know as soon as I can."

Sally was at Liz's gallery. She assured Meg that she'd be more than happy to arrive the next evening so that Meg could get an early start the following day. Meg called Amy back to confirm. She looked at the calendar as she hung up the phone; it was only the twelfth of January, but for Meg it felt as if this dreadful month was actually reaching an end.

Meg sang along with the radio as she drove. She felt just a little guilty at leaving Fang and Brandy for a whole week, but she knew that they'd be content with Sally's care. Meg's spirits lifted as she reached the Thruway. Perhaps another hour until she hit the traffic leading into the city. She'd be at Amy's apartment by noon. Amy would be up and about, she'd said, getting ready for her waitressing shift at two. She'd be working until ten, so Meg would have the apartment to herself. When Amy got home, she'd said, they could make some tentative plans for getting together with Brian and Jerry while Meg was in town.

Meg hung two dresses in the hall closet and then stashed her suitcase in a corner of the bathroom. "I didn't want to share on a permanent basis," Amy said apologetically. "This is really tiny, but I can afford it by myself."

Meg looked around the small apartment. One L-shaped room served as bedroom (when Amy's futon was open) and living room. A tiny kitchen looked as if it had been made from a closet. But the floors were parquet, and the huge windows let the sun stream in. Amy's paintings lined the walls and overflowed into stacks in the hallway that led to the bathroom. "I like it," Meg said. "Thanks for letting me stay here."

"So what are your plans for today?" Amy asked. "Are you meeting that good-looking Erik?"

Meg hesitated, then blurted out, "I didn't let him know that I was coming early."

Amy raised an eyebrow and Meg continued, "It's over, Amy. I'm going to see him and let him know. I thought I'd do that this evening. I'll be taking some paintings around to Calloway's this afternoon, hoping to get Diane Calloway to reconsider representing my work. Maybe when I'm finished there I'll just go on over to Erik's apartment and get this over with."

"So you'll really be at loose ends after tonight. I'll

call Jerry when I get home tonight, and we'll see what we can set up for tomorrow. I know that Brian will be happy to see you. He seems to have adopted you, you know."

Meg winced inwardly as she recognized the little sister/big brother attitude that she'd forced herself to accept. She managed a small smile. "I'll be glad to see him again, Amy. And, as I told Liz, I'll be happy to take my turn at baby-sitting Michael during the day."

Meg brewed herself a cup of coffee and foraged in the refrigerator and found some yogurt (which she promised herself to replace). The small lunch wiped away the last of the weariness from the drive. She changed from her jeans into her little black dress and drove the few blocks to Calloway's Gallery.

Diane smothered her in a hug and kissed the air on either side of her head, the typical New York greeting. "Where have you been, Meg dear?" she gushed. "I've sold the last of your wildflowers and wondered when you would bring me more."

"But—" Meg began. She caught herself, her mind racing. "I wasn't sure that you were ready for more," she said, trying to keep her statements ambiguous. "I've been changing with the seasons, Diane. Right now it's snowstorm pictures. Would you like to see them?"

"But of course," the gallery owner said. "Go get your car, and double-park in front as usual. Beep the horn and I'll come out and see how many I can take."

Meg's thoughts churned wildly as she walked around the corner to where she had parked her car.

She couldn't have misunderstood Sharon; she remembered the conversation all too clearly. Why would her friend deliberately mislead her?

Diane gushed over the paintings and finally decided that she had room to hang them all. That would certainly come as a surprise to Sharon, Meg thought. She stayed for a little while, on eye on her double-parked car, and made small talk with Diane as they shared a cup of coffee. Diane loved to talk, and Meg appreciated the chance to catch up on the trends in the New York art scene.

Once back in the car she allowed herself time to think. She drove aimlessly until she reached the Battery, then pulled into the nearly vacant public parking lot and put her head down on the steering wheel. One of her best friends had attempted to sabotage her career—the very same best friend who had stepped in to fill the job that Meg had turned down. Meg hadn't expected thanks, but neither had she expected betrayal. Surely Sharon didn't think that Meg would decide to return to New York and want the job for herself, and surely she didn't think that Diane Calloway would just welcome her back even if she did. It didn't make sense.

Sharon and Erik? Could the night at the ballet mean something more than two old acquaintances spending an evening together? If Sharon were interested in Erik, would she attempt to make certain that Meg would have no gallery contact in the city and thus no reason to come down to New York? It seemed farfetched. Surely Sharon would realize that Meg would just try to make arrangements with another gallery. Surely she would think that Meg would come to the city just to see Erik, even if no gallery were showing her paintings. Surely that was so . . . and yet, weeks had gone by and Meg had not come down to see Erik, had not worked up her courage to search for a new gallery. She had almost let Sharon get away with her little scheme.

Unless this was all imagination. Meg forced herself back from her premature suspicions. There might well be some other reason for Sharon's lie, a reason that made at least as much sense as the scheme that Meg was imagining.

She glanced at her watch. 5:30. Well, it was time to face Erik, unannounced and two days early.

Meg shut her eyes and rang the doorbell. "Surprise," she said.

Erik looked stunned when he opened the door.

"Who is it?" came a familiar voice from the kitchen. Sharon walked into the living room, looking very domestic in her frilly apron.

"Well," Meg said, finding herself at a loss for words.

"Well," Erik echoed. He looked back and forth from the woman in the hall to the woman in the kitchen doorway, clearly unable to think of what to say.

"Dinner's ready, Erik," Sharon said. "I'm sorry we can't ask you to join us, Meg, but I cooked just enough for two. If you would pour the wine," she said as she walked over to Erik and put her hand on his arm.

He looked from one of them to the other again. "I'll call you," he yelled after Meg as she ran out the door and down the stairs.

Chapter Thirteen

"So she scuttled your gallery connection and then stole your boyfriend. Some friend!"

"There must be some explanation, Amy. Maybe she thought that I didn't care about Erik. Liz said that I sometimes gave that impression. And, of course, it turns out to be true. That's what is so ironic about all this."

"And she thought you didn't care about Calloway's Gallery either? Get real, Meg. Your old buddy is a first-class snake. And I'm sure that your Erik isn't any real loss."

Meg was spared the necessity of a comment by the ringing of the phone. "Speak of the devil," Amy said after listening for a minute to the impassioned pleading from the other end of the line. "Erik for you," she said with a smug smile as she handed over the phone.

"I can explain, Meg," he said.

"How did you find me? My dear friend Sharon didn't know where I was staying, and I don't remember giving you Amy's number."

"I called your house. I figured you'd have somebody there with the animals. I did the 'I was supposed to call her but I've lost the number' routine. I guess I sounded convincing. Now if I could only sound as convincing when I try to explain to you."

"I'm not sure there's anything to explain, Erik. I don't own you. You're free to go out with Sharon— to become involved with Sharon . . ."

"I'm not involved with Sharon. She just seems to have moved in to my life. She volunteers to cook dinner, she comes up with tickets to shows, she calls and says she's found a great new restaurant . . ."

"And she ties you up and drags you off to all these places?"

"I'm not pleading innocence, Meg. I could have discouraged her at any time. But it was something to do, and better than sitting home thinking about you or pretending to be making progress on my novel."

Meg didn't know what to say, so she said nothing at all.

"Meg? Are you still there? Sharon doesn't mean anything special to me. She's an interesting companion, but that's all."

Meg took a deep breath. "Erik, I came to New York because I wanted to talk to you. I didn't want to do it over the phone, but now I think I'd just better say what's on my mind. I don't see a future for us."

It was Erik's turn to be at a loss for words. There

was a prolonged silence, and then he muttered, "I guess I saw this coming. Ever since you moved to Bennington . . ."

"It was coming whether I moved to Bennington or not. Being there just gave me a chance to put things in perspective."

"You sound as if you've really made a decision."

"I have, Erik. I think it's for the best. I'm glad you have Sharon."

He choked a little but wished her luck. When she hung up the phone she felt better than she had in a long time.

"Hi, Julia." Meg was beginning to enjoy the shock on the faces of her old friends.

Julia looked as if she'd like to hide behind the counter of MOMA's gift shop. "Meg! I didn't know that you were still going to be in town. I mean . . ."

"I know exactly what you mean, Julia. You thought that if I couldn't stay with you and Sharon that I'd just give up and remain in Bennington. Just like Sharon believed that if I thought that Calloway's didn't want my paintings I'd just give up trying to sell them in New York."

"Calloway's? I don't understand."

Meg studied Julia's face for evidence of the lie. "You don't know what Sharon's been up to?" she asked.

Julia blushed. "I know what she's been up to, all right. I'm sorry to have been a part of it, Meg. But I have to live with her, you know, at least until our lease ends in May. I've been looking for another apartment to move into then. I've been saving my money; I think

I can afford a studio by myself." She reached her hand out toward Meg, then drew it back. "Anyway, I'm sorry that I went along with the lie. Of course there are no out-of-town friends in our apartment. You're absolutely right—Sharon thought that you'd just give up on making this trip if she threw a stumbling block in your way. She's been making a big fool of herself over Erik. She thinks that he's really becoming interested, though I think she's kidding herself."

"Maybe he really will become interested in Sharon," Meg said. "I just told him that it was all over between us. That had nothing to do with Sharon, by the way." She paused and looked hard at Julia. "But what about the Calloway's scheme?"

"I don't know what you're talking about, Meg." Julia looked at her watch. "Listen, if you're not too angry with me, let's have lunch. I'm off in ten minutes. You can tell me what's going on at Calloway's—and fill me in on what went wrong between you and Erik."

Meg browsed through the museum gift shop, happy enough to have the ten minutes in which to gather her thoughts. Julia didn't seem to be in the enemy camp. It would be good to have one more friend in the city, someone she could count on in addition to Amy and Jerry.

"Is the museum restaurant all right?" Julia appeared at Meg's side. She looked extremely fashionable in her dark green suede dress, with her red hair gathered up in a sleek topknot. Meg glanced down at her own black dress, one of her very few dresses, she realized. One of the advantages of working at Bennington instead of in the city.

Julia waited until they had placed the order. "What's

this about Calloway's?" she asked then. "I remember from when we were at Brian's friend's apartment— what was his name?—that you said they didn't want your paintings."

"It wasn't true, Julia." Meg could still scarcely believe the whole thing herself. "Sharon caught me that day before I ever set foot in the gallery and told me that Diane was concentrating on two new artists—city-scapes—and didn't feel that my work would fit into her plans for the foreseeable future. Of course I believed her. It never occurred to me to check with Diane herself. But I decided to try again on this trip. I thought that perhaps the new artists hadn't worked out, or that they'd been such a success that their works were all sold. And I had these great storm paintings that I really felt Diane would like. So I went to the gallery yesterday, actually expecting to see Sharon, and Diane greeted me as if I'd risen from the dead. She'd wondered what happened to me, why I hadn't brought her anything for such a long time."

"There's no way you could have misunderstood what Sharon said?"

"I've been trying to think back, looking for some other interpretation. But it was pretty clear, Julia. I have to face the fact that this was another attempt to convince me to stay in Bennington."

"Wow," Julia said. "Some friend."

"I can understand, at least a little, why she might try this last lie—why she might not want me staying in your apartment if she was trying to get Erik for herself. But I can't understand how she could be mean enough to sabotage my artistic career. That's serious stuff, Julia."

"For sure." Julia's green eyes looked troubled. "Did you explain to Diane?"

"No. I didn't know quite what to say. I stumbled around a little, but I think I just sounded vague. The scatterbrained artist bit."

"If Diane knew that Sharon had done that to you— and to the gallery as well, actually—she'd probably fire her. Boy, would that serve her right! You'd probably be offered the job again, Meg. Not that you want it, of course. I know how happy you've been in Bennington."

Meg shook her head. "I couldn't do that to Sharon."

"Couldn't do that to Sharon? You're trying for saint of the month? Look at what she did to you."

"What she did to me isn't permanent, Julia. My paintings are back at Calloway's. What I decided about Erik had nothing to do with Sharon. For his sake, I'm glad she stepped in to fill the gap. But if I told Diane Calloway what Sharon had done . . . you're probably right. Diane would fire her. And what would be her chances of getting another gallery job? Word gets around. I wouldn't want to feel responsible for that."

"But revenge is so sweet."

"I don't think Sharon was actually trying to hurt me, Julia. I don't think she thought that far ahead. I think it was a spur-of-the-moment decision."

"You're being naive, Meg. If it was a spontaneous decision, she could have undone it after she'd had time to think about it. She could have called you in two weeks and said that Diane wanted to see more paintings the next time you were in town."

Meg bit her lip. "It doesn't matter now, Julia. Let's talk about something else now. How's your love life?"

Julia claimed that there were no men in New York that interested her. She pried for information about "that hunk," as she called Brian. Meg admitted that he was in New York, and that Liz was back in Bennington. She made it clear that Brian and Liz were a couple and finally got around to telling Julia about Brian's child. Julia, undiscouraged, still insisted that they should all get together while Meg was in town. Meg promised to try to arrange an evening with Jerry and Amy and Brian.

Meg sat on the futon and watched as Amy rummaged in the small closet, trying to decide what to wear. Amy said over her shoulder, "Forgive me if I butt into something that isn't any of my business, Meg, but exactly what are your feelings toward Brian? I've seen the way you look at him when his back is turned."

Meg blushed, happy that Amy had turned back to scrutinize the closet. "Brian belongs to Liz," she muttered, knowing that she hadn't answered the question.

Amy turned around and burst out laughing. "You must be the only one who thinks that."

Meg's face showed her confusion. "They're always together. I've barely ever seen Brian without her."

"But you'd like to?"

Meg ignored Amy's question and asked one of her own. "What makes you think they're *not* a couple?"

"Liz and Jerry are Brian's best friends. Jerry and I have known Brian and Liz for ages. Their relationship hasn't changed since she was his student. They became good friends almost right away, and they've remained good friends through the years. We've never thought of it as a romance, and we're certainly with them often enough to know. They stay at our apartment when they're in the city, and I've never even seen him kiss her except on the cheek."

"But . . ."

"But what? You still haven't answered my question, Meg. How do *you* feel about Brian?" Meg was quiet, staring off into space. "I have to go to work now," Amy said. "Don't think I'm going to stop asking the question, though, Meg." Amy waved good bye as she headed off to her job.

"I think he's wonderful," Meg whispered to herself. She sat back with a sigh. Brian. She'd convinced Julia that she couldn't have Brian because he belonged to Liz. But if he didn't?

There were two extra men at Jerry's apartment, in addition to the unattached-for-the-night Brian. Meg wondered if one of them had been earmarked for her. Julia seemed to have reconciled herself to Brian's unavailability and appeared to be weighing the relative merits of the two new possibilities.

Brian hugged Meg enthusiastically. "I've missed you, Meg," he said. "I'm not sure I miss all that snow you've been having in Vermont, though."

"The snow has accounted for some great paintings," Meg said. She tried not to think about how that casual hug had made her feel. "And Diane Calloway wanted them all on consignment. So I have nothing stacked on the sunporch at homer except some fall foliage pictures, left over from when I thought Calloway's was done with me. I'm almost eager to get home and get to work on spring scenes. It will be time to start forcing forsythia and apple blossoms."

Meg tried to make light of Sharon's duplicity in response to Brian's questions about exactly what had happened at Calloway's Gallery. She avoided any reference to her old friend's attempt to steal Erik. It no longer mattered, and it was best forgotten.

Jerry and Brian talked animatedly about the play, now in its second week with Brian in the lead. Brian seemed thrilled to be on stage for a change. The little group made plans to see the play on the weekend. Meg wondered which of the spare men Julia would latch on to—or if she would just happily consider both of them, plus Brian, to be her escorts. Meg couldn't help daydreaming. Brian was not involved with Liz. Maybe someday he would be ready to love again.

Chapter Fourteen

Meg steered Michael around the huge rink on his double-runners. She could almost remember her own first struggling efforts to glide over the ice. "Skating, Meg," he shouted. "I'm skating!"

She skated over toward the edge of the rink with him. "Stand right there for a minute and let me take a picture to show your dad," she said.

"Picture for Daddy," he echoed. "Daddy can see me skate."

"We'll surprise your daddy," Meg said as she snapped the picture. "We'll bring him along with us on his next free day."

"Daddy skate too?"

Meg thought of Brian, growing up in the South, living in Bennington for . . . how many years? Six, she remembered. "I don't know," she said. "Maybe you'll have to teach him." Michael giggled at the thought,

137

and Meg took his elbow to guide him in another turn around the enormous rink. "We can skate when we're back home, too," she said. "I'll take you and Robbie someday, to the pond behind the college."

"Robbie skate too?" Michael was clearly fascinated with this new idea that maybe everyone could skate.

"Probably not. His mom will have to get him some skates, and we'll have to teach him. Maybe his mom will come too, if she can get a baby-sitter for Carrie."

"Angela skate? Carrie skate?"

Meg smiled at the thought of the six-month-old baby, double runners fastened to her well-padded bottom. "Angela probably knows how to skate," she said. "Carrie is too little. Babies can't skate."

"Only big boys, like Robbie and me," Michael said proudly. "Let me try it myself now, Meg."

Meg watched as he tried a few hesitant steps. "Slide," she yelled. "You can't try to walk." She took his elbow again and showed him what she was doing with her own feet. He set off by himself again, this time managing a small imitation of the sliding motion. "That's it," she shouted after him as he made his way along the side of the rink. "That's it, Michael. You're skating!"

Meg took Michael back to Army's apartment with her, Brian and Jerry were coming for dinner, so there was no point in delivering the exhausted child to Jerry's apartment only to have him bundled off and brought to Amy's later. She made hot chocolate; the ritual reminded her of her own mother, of skating on the very pond where she had promised Michael they'd go . . . when? . . . next winter? It wouldn't be this year, she realized. Brian and Michael would be in New York until spring.

She put the requisite marshmallow in the mug and set it down in front of Michael. He poked at it with his spoon, making it dive under the liquid and pop up again, just as Meg remembered doing when she was a child. She opened a can of spaghetti—horrid stuff, she thought, but all she could find at the market this morning when she realized that she'd need something quick to feed a hungry child. She spooned the orangey mess into a bowl and put it in the microwave. The bell dinged, and she stirred and tasted, verifying that it was not too hot.

"Getti," Michael said. He reached for the bowl with a big smile.

Meg got Michael into his pajamas and settled him on Amy's futon. She picked up one of his storybooks that Brian had thoughtfully packed for him, and was only partway through the escapades of *The Cat in the Hat* when sleepy eyes closed. Meg yawned. It had been years since she'd been ice-skating, and the exercise and the cold had taken their toll on her, too. She glanced at her watch—5:00. She curled up next to the sleeping child, thankful that she had at least two hours for a nap before the other adults arrived.

"Shhh," she said, finger to lip, as Amy let herself and the men into the apartment.

"Did you drug him?" Brian asked. "I usually have trouble getting him to fall asleep by seven or eight."

"You'll be sorry tomorrow morning when he wakes

up at six," Meg replied, "but I guess I really tired him out. We've been ice-skating. I promised him that you'd come with us on your next free day."

"Oh, thanks, Meg."

"I told Michael that you might not know how, seeing as how you're a Southern boy. He thought that was very funny."

"We could all go," Amy said. "That way at least there would be three adults who know how to skate— one to help Michael, and two to hold Brian on his feet."

"And what other activities to you have planned for us, Meg?" Brian asked with a twinkle in his eye. "Something that I know how to do, I hope."

"How about tobogganing?" she asked.

Brian groaned. "How about something that doesn't involve snow?"

"I was joking about the tobogganing. We need serious hills for that, bigger than what we can find in the city. That will have to wait till next winter, back at Bennington. But surely you want to take advantage of the snow. How about sledding in the park?"

"I can handle that. Michael and Robbie and I sled on the hill behind the college. You know, though, Meg, that the fieldwork-term students trek up to Central Park with him at least once a week. He's not sledding-deprived. Anyway, you don't have to play baby-sitter. The students have been doing it, and it was working out all right."

Meg tried to decide what he meant. Was he telling her to back off? Did he see her time with his son as some scheme to become closer to him? And was it exactly that? "I'm enjoying it, Brian," she said coldly. "But if I'm messing up the students' schedule I'll find another way to amuse myself."

"Meg, I just don't want you to feel that he's your responsibility. You came to New York to see your own friends, not to baby-sit my son."

"I have plenty of time for both," she replied, still not certain whether or not her help was wanted. She changed the subject by asking about the play.

She tried to erase the image from her mind—of the huge, bearlike Brian with two small boys in front of him on the sled, flying down the Bennington hill that she remembered so well. She was willing to admit that she loved little Michael, but she reminded herself that she knew better than to fall in love with his father. She might have daydreams about a future with Brian, but it was pretty clear that he didn't think that his future involved her.

Friday afternoon while Brian was in rehearsal Meg and Michael built a snowman in Washington Square Park. Michael delighted in pushing the big ball of snow, rolling it over and over (with Meg's help) until it was nearly as tall as his chest. Then they made the second ball. By then some NYU students had joined in the fun. They decided that the bottom ball of snow should be even bigger, so they continued to roll it until it was about three feet around. They hoisted the first ball that Michael had made on top of the new, larger one, and then the smallest ball on top of that. "Snowman!" Michael chortled.

One of the students broke off a dried branch from

a nearby tree. He fashioned a blob of snow and stuck it to the side of the snowman, then put the branch in the creature's "hand."

Meg was sorry that she hadn't planned ahead a little better. The snowman had no hat, no scarf, no eyes or nose or mouth. The students also seemed to feel that something was missing. The one who had added the hand came back with another branch. He broke it into pieces, using stubs for eyes, a curvy length pressed sideways into the snow for the mouth, a blunt piece sticking out for the nose. They all stepped back to admire their handiwork.

Meg took a picture of Michael next to the snowman. "Show Daddy?" he asked.

"Yes, we'll show Daddy," she said.

"Daddy and Michael and Robbie make snowman."

She couldn't figure out whether this was a request or a news report. "When?" she asked.

Michael looked puzzled. Meg waited, wondering how to rephrase the question. "I was little," he said.

Last winter. She pictured Brian playing in the snow with the two little boys. He'd said that they'd been sledding, too. *We'll do that again*, she thought, *next winter in Bennington.* She realized suddenly that she was assuming a next year—that she was assuming her teaching assistant's contract would be renewed and that her life would continue much as it was. Dinner and movies with Liz and Brian, or sometimes with Sally, whichever of her crowd were still around. Romps in the meadow with Michael and Brandy. The fun in the winter snow and the beauty of the spring thaw. The breathtaking colors of the autumn leaves.

She took Michael's hand as they walked back to

Jerry's apartment. It would be another night with an early bedtime, she suspected. Tomorrow was Saturday. There would be no rehearsal. It would be a good time to go ice-skating again, this time with Brian and Amy and Jerry.

"What if I break a leg?" Brian asked. "Jerry's already lost one leading man because of an accident."

Amy giggled. "Isn't 'break a leg' what actors tell each other just before they go on stage? I always thought it was something that you all wanted to do."

"I'd just have to play the lead myself," Jerry said. "You're all against me!"

"Daddy skate?"

"Yes, Daddy will skate. Just remember, all of you," he said to the three adults, "you promised to hold me up."

It did seem strange to take a subway to go ice-skating. Michael chattered the whole way, mostly about how he knew how to skate and his daddy didn't.

"I'd hoped they would be all out of my size," Brian said as they collected their rental skates and sat on the bench to lace them up.

Michael took off at once on his double runners, eager to show his father what he'd learned earlier in the week. "Slide," Meg reminded him.

Jerry and Meg reached for Brian's arms, but he twisted away and glided over the ice. He did a smooth turn and skated backward around the huge rink. He made another fancy twist and came to a picture-perfect stop in front of his amazed friends.

"I thought you didn't know how to skate," Amy exclaimed as she clapped her mittened hands.

"I never said that," Brian said.

They all thought back to the conversations they'd had. Meg took the blame. "I said that you might not know how, and you didn't say anything to correct me."

"Daddy skate!" Michael shouted as he slipped and slid to where the others stood.

Brian scooped his small son into his arms and soared around the rink.

"Yes," Amy said admiringly, "Daddy skate."

They bought hot dogs from a street vendor and trudged back to the subway. Michael's head was nodding by the time they reached the stop for Jerry's apartment. The fresh air had left everybody ready for an afternoon nap, so Amy and Meg stayed on for two more stops and hiked the few blocks to Amy's place.

"You never answered my question," Amy said when they had settled down with their steaming-hot coffee.

"What question?"

"You know. How do you feel about Brian?"

"I just love little Michael," Meg volunteered with a cheery smile.

"I was asking about the *daddy*."

"I'm not going to let myself think about it," Meg admitted. "The better question might be how Brian feels about me. Somehow I think he's a long way from being ready to love again."

Chapter Fifteen

Meg was happy to be home. It seemed as if she'd been gone much longer than a week. She fed Brandy and Fang, even though she knew that Sally had taken care of that chore just that morning. She called the gallery to tell Liz and Sally that she was back. They made plans to watch a video at Meg's house that night.

It seemed as if there had been another foot of snow in the week she'd been gone, but perhaps it was just that she was comparing it to New York. She let Brandy out, watching from the sunporch as the big dog rolled in the snow. Fang watched, too, and Meg could almost believe that there was a disdainful expression on the cat's face.

Meg unpacked and did a load of laundry. She wandered through the house, running her hand over the antique furniture that she loved. She'd rewaxed the floors after the burst-pipe flood, and the old random-

145

width pine looked mellow in the afternoon sunlight that poured in the big windows. Home. This was really home.

The dog came in through the kitchen door and shook herself vigorously. Meg mopped up the wet spots cheerfully. In some ways animals were like children—the joy they brought more than made up for the messes they sometimes caused.

She took inventory of the paintings on the sunporch. Diane Calloway said that she knew she could take two more snow scenes in another couple of weeks, and she'd like some spring flowers soon after that. As soon as the snow was gone, Meg told herself, she'd have to cut some bare branches of the forsythia that grew near the garage. The snow should be gone by . . . when? Meg couldn't quite remember. Often enough there was a heavy, wet snowfall in early April, but surely during the last weeks of February—or at least by March—she would see bare ground—again at least for a little while.

The daylight was nearly gone by late afternoon. This was the time of year to settle down by the fireplace with a good book—or, like tonight, with a video and good friends. Meg rooted in the freezer, trying to decide what would be good for supper. It was well stocked. She'd vowed that she'd stay prepared for whatever the tag-end of this winter might bring. She probably wouldn't have to shop until spring.

She turned to the shelves lining the stairway to the basement and reached for the last jar of homemade soup. Her mother's carefully preserved foods were nearly gone. It felt like the end of an era.

She ate the soup, took a shower, and put on an old

sweatsuit. She had at least another hour until Sally and Liz arrived. She sat down at the piano and sang along as she played old songs, ending with "Galway Bay."

It seemed strange to be back on campus and know that she wouldn't be running into Brian. But now she had new friends: Sally, Valerie, Ruth, Rachael, and Connie. She met them for lunch at the Commons on the days when she had classes both morning and afternoon. On other days, she usually convinced Liz to close the gallery for half an hour and grab a bite with her in town.

She tried to get Liz to talk about Brian and occasionally managed some small success. "I thought that you and Brian were a couple," Meg admitted one day over sandwiches and coffee.

Liz choked on her sandwich. "I love Brian, but as a brother," she said after half a glass of water had enabled her to recover. "Remember, when I met him he was married to Laurie. I got used to thinking of him as just a friend, and our relationship has just never changed. Besides—if and when I become part of a couple, it will be with someone who doesn't come with quite so much baggage!"

"Baggage? You mean Michael?"

"Children aren't my thing, in case you hadn't guessed. My career is important to me, and I don't want to put it on hold. I love the kid, and he wouldn't present a problem; it won't be long before he'll be off to school. But Brian and Laurie had planned on a big family, and I know that wasn't all Laurie's idea. Brian's life was going just the way he wanted it to— until the accident. And that's the baggage I'm talking about." She ticked her points off on her fingers. "One: men who idolized their ex-wives usually can't find anyone else who quite measures up. Two: and that's even if they've laid wife number one to rest, and I'm not sure that Brian has."

Meg chewed her sandwich thoughtfully. She swallowed and said, "You're right, Liz. There's too much baggage. You'd have to be really crazy to get involved with him."

Liz grinned. "I'm pretty certain that you've been in love with Brian for a long time. You just haven't admitted it to yourself. Sometimes, Meg, love makes fools of us all."

Meg told herself that she was going to New York just because Diane Calloway was ready for more paintings. It had nothing to do, she insisted, with the fact that she'd see Brian. Still, she found herself thinking that if Calloway's wanted new works every couple of weeks, she'd spend almost as much time with him as when he was in Bennington. That was nonsense, she knew. If he were in Bennington, she'd be eating lunch with him twice a week and spending an evening or two with him and Liz. And once a month might be a better guess for taking paintings to Diane.

She'd faced up to the fact that she loved Brian, but she'd reconciled herself to appreciating him as a friend. One thing she'd learned during the harsh winter was that she could rely on herself. She had a job that she loved, her painting was going well, she was cozy and content in her own house with Brandy and Fang. She had friends, and she'd be happy to have Brian back in town and part of that group. Once in a while she fantasized about being a mother to Michael and several other rusty-haired children, but she knew that she could build a life of her own whether or not that dream ever came true. Someday the right person would come into her life. She hoped it was Brian, but she wasn't counting on it.

She'd cut the forsythia and the apple branches, taking advantage of a February thaw which melted the snow and left the fields muddy and rutted. She heaped the bare branches into great tubs of water on the sunporch. Now she could see the swollen buds beginning to form, a promise of spring. Maybe by the time she got back from this trip she could begin the paintings that would herald the new season.

Meg loaded the last of the winter storm pictures into the trunk of her car. Sally had the house key. She was always happy to escape the dorm for the weekend, so she'd come tonight to stay with Brandy and Fang until Meg returned.

Meg would be staying with Amy. Julia had remained a staunch friend, but Meg had no desire to spend any more time with Sharon than she had to— and she was certain that the feeling was mutual. She'd see her when she dropped her stuff at Calloway's, of course, but she could manage to remain cool and professional during that brief time.

Tonight she'd see Jerry's play again. She never tired of seeing Brian on stage. Amy, who had seen the play more times than she could count, was the baby-sitter for the evening. Afterward they'd gather in Jerry's apartment until the wee hours, or until Meg, who was not on the same night-owl schedule as the others, pleaded that her eyes would no longer stay open.

She sang as she crossed the Tappan Zee bridge. Her life was almost perfect.

"Interesting news," Brian said when she met him in the Green Room after the show. "Tony will be taking over again at the end of March."

Meg looked blank.

"Tony. He was in an accident; I got the part. Now he's nearly ready to come back."

"Oh." That meant Brian would be coming home. "How do you feel about that?"

"I'm glad for Tony. For a while they thought he'd never walk again. But he surprised them all, worked on his therapy like a demon, and he can manage now with crutches. Jerry's pretty committed to the idea that crutches can't matter in the portrayal of this character. That's a real break for Tony. It gets him back on stage sooner than he could have hoped. It's good for everybody, really, when the disabled are treated as just regular people."

"And how do you feel about it for you?"

He grinned. "I won't deny that it's been a thrill. It's easy to get caught up in the applause. But I never planned to be an actor. I'm a playwright—and it's time I got back to writing."

"It's the middle of the term. There won't be any teaching duties open."

"They'll give me a tutorial or two. And it's a good time to round up some juniors, get them started on their senior theses a little early. I don't need to be back to full-time pay. I'll have made enough money here by the end of March to tide me over until I'm teaching again in the July program, or even until next fall if

I'm in New York for the summer. And I can spend time with Michael. It's been pretty hard with the heavy rehearsal and performance schedule to be with him as much as I'd like. During January that wasn't a problem; he was really the Little Prince as far as the fieldwork-term students were concerned. Now, though, the students are all back at Bennington. We're settling for all day at nursery school, with Amy baby-sitting when she's not working and scrounging for sitters when she is. I'll be really happy to have some extra time for him."

"Meg!" Michael launched himself toward her, hitting her at the knees as he wrapped his arms around her. "You're here! Can we go skating?"

She turned to Brian. "No one has taken him skating since I was here last? Poor, deprived child."

"We have him convinced that you're the only one who knows how to get to Rockefeller Center. Clever of us, wasn't it?"

She bent down and ruffled the coppery hair. "Sure, Mike. Tomorrow morning, bright and early, before your father's even out of bed. But that means you have to go to bed soon. You wouldn't want to be too sleepy to get up tomorrow."

He looked at her soberly and nodded. "Pajamas now, Dad," he directed.

"I wish I could get him to bed this easily every night," Brian said as he picked up his small son and tossed him, giggling, over his shoulder.

"All you have to do is promise to take him skating early in the morning," Meg called after him.

"Morning. Not to be faced before noon," Jerry quipped.

Meg found some crackers in the cupboard and rummaged in the refrigerator until she found some cheese. She put it all on a plate and set it on the coffee table. "Good start," Amy said. "But how about if we call out for Chinese?"

"The wonders of the big city," Meg said. "I can't imagine what I could call out for at eleven at night back in Bennington."

"But you and Brian have the best of both worlds," Jerry said. "You get to live in Bennington, but you're here often enough to get your city-fix."

Brian walked back into the room just in time to hear the last comment. "It's certainly the best of both worlds," he agreed with a wry smile. "It's as good as my world is going to get."

Meg drove home with a heavy heart. She could see all too clearly that Liz was right. Brian wasn't ready to find happiness again—either with her or with anyone else.

She cheered up when she opened the door to be greeted by Brandy and Fang. The buds on the branches on the sunporch were just ready to burst. It was the end of February. In another month Brian and Michael would be home, and spring would be just around the corner. She and Liz and Brian would be a threesome again, sharing dinners and movies. She reminded herself that she didn't need Brian's love in order to be happy, but she hoped that he might someday be happy, too.

Chapter Sixteen

Meg bit on the paintbrush which she had clutched between her teeth as she studied her attempt to capture the forsythia. Another heavy snow had driven all thoughts of spring from her mind, but crocus would soon be in bloom in the city. This was the time for Diane to sell these paintings that spoke of spring— now, when the small piles of snow that remained in New York would be pushed into dirty mounds along the gutters. If she could finish this painting today, and the apple blossoms by the weekend, she could drive down on Wednesday and deliver them to the gallery. But this attempt seemed flat and uninteresting.

Fang wrapped himself around her legs. Meg was seized by inspiration. The cat wouldn't pose, of course, but . . . She picked him up and stroked him soothingly. She muttered sweet words into his ear as she carried him into the den and picked up her camera.

153

She walked back to the sunporch and put the cat on the table next to the tub of flowers. He sat there and looked at her as if he wondered what she had in mind. *I may be sorry for this later,* she thought as she wiggled a branch of forsythia. She moved away, and Fang reached a tentative paw toward the elusive branch. She snapped the picture. The cat stood up and put both paws on the edge of the pot and buried his nose in the blossoms. She shot again. *Any minute now he'll upset the whole tub*, she thought, *and every bouquet I bring into the house ever again*. But the little cat backed away, stared at the branches, then reached out and batted one with his paw. Another picture. Meg kept shooting until the cat tired of the game.

She drove the film to the pharmacy that promised one-hour development, then went back home and prepared a fresh canvas. "You're going to be famous," she said to the cat.

Two hours later she had the charcoal sketch done. Then she worked nonstop with her oils until she knew that only finishing touches were needed. "That's enough for the day," she said to her little family who waited patiently for supper. She stood back and studied the painting of the cat reaching for the forsythia branch. "Too cute," she said. "Too Norman Rockwell. But I think it will walk right out the gallery door."

Diane gushed over "Fang with Forsythia," as Meg had come to call the painting. "Not great art, hon," she said. "Actually, pure kitsch. But it will sell. Bring me more!"

Meg headed to Amy's apartment in high spirits. She had a key now, but of course she always called ahead to let Amy know when she was coming. She knocked when she arrived, never certain what Amy's waitressing hours might be.

"Come in," Brian yelled. Michael, in his little footed pajamas, ran to her when she walked in the door. She picked him up and swung him around, then dropped him on his father's lap where he sat cross-legged on the floor. She leaned over and kissed Brian lightly, then hugged Amy and Jerry.

"Looks as if I'm just in time for the party. Are we celebrating something?"

"We move to a bigger theater next week. It's beginning to look like a really long run."

"Oh, Jerry, that's just great!"

"And," Amy said shyly, "we've decided that we can afford to get married. Tomorrow, actually. I'm glad you're here, Meg. I hope you'll be a bridesmaid. The wedding will just be at city hall. We may have a more formal ceremony and reception back in my hometown when the play reaches the end of its run—but of course we hope that won't be for a long time."

"Good thing I brought a dress in case I went to a concert," Meg said. She hugged her friend again, harder this time. "This is so exciting!" She thought for a minute. "Liz will be sorry she missed this."

"We called her, just before you arrived," Jerry said. "Yes, she threatened never to speak to us again unless we postponed the wedding until next week when she could be here. But we ignored her. Finally she said that she'd call Sally, close the shop, and be here by noon tomorrow to act as maid of honor. Too bad we didn't get this organized a little sooner so that the two of you could have driven down together. We've had the license for a month, but it was only this afternoon that we really decided that tomorrow was the day."

"What needs to be done? Flowers? Cake?"

"We didn't think we needed—"

"I'll take care of it." Meg was out the door and down the stairs before Amy had a chance to protest any further.

Meg looked up and down the street. It might have been a good idea to check the yellow pages before she barged out of the apartment. Still, it was possible to find anything in the Village at almost any hour. She didn't even think she'd need to retrieve her car from the car park. She headed off toward the nearest little clump of stores where she picked up food whenever she stayed with Amy. She thought she remembered a flower shop just a few doors past the little grocery.

She congratulated herself on her memory as the florist's sign came in sight. It was easy to decide what to buy. It had to be already on hand, and it had to coordinate with her new mauve-colored dress. Liz would need a corsage. Meg wondered what her friend would wear. She settled on gardenias for the bride. White roses would be safe enough for Liz and would be perfect with her own dress, too. Jerry and Brian got little white rosebuds for their buttonholes. She remembered just in time that Michael would want a boutonniere, too, just like the big boys. She arranged to pick everything up in the morning, since Amy's refrigerator space was too limited for overnight flower storage.

The florist knew of a bakery, just three blocks down and one block over. The friendly proprietor saw no trouble in having a small wedding cake ready by the next day. Meg was proud of herself as she walked the few blocks back to Amy's apartment. For a last-minute bridesmaid, she thought she'd done pretty well.

Liz must have left almost at first light, because it was only 10:00 when she arrived. The men and Michael were back in Jerry's apartment. *Good thing*, Meg thought, trying to imagine the chaos of five adults and one child getting into their wedding clothes in a studio apartment. Even with three women there had to be careful planning, with much patience while waiting for the bathroom or for a mirror. Meg saw that Liz's dress was green, and congratulated herself on the choice of white roses. Amy had found—literally, she said, at one of her favorite consignment shops—an off-white silk shantung sheath.

"I'll get dressed last," Meg said. "I'll pick up the flowers and the cake. I'd better buy a disposable camera, too. I'll get my car, stop at the bakery, pick up the flowers, go to the drug store for a camera, double-park here to unload, then take the car back to the car park. It should take about an hour. When I get back, the bathtub is mine!"

"I brought a camera," Liz yelled from the bathroom. "That means one less stop. And I'm not sure you should return your car to the car park. We'll need either your car or mine to get to city hall," Liz said. "Brian's won't hold all of us."

"No," Amy said. "There won't be any place to park. I think we may need to spring for a couple of cabs. I'd suggest the subway, but I know I'd be outvoted."

"It's a good thing we're not talking church wedding here," Meg said to Liz as they finally climbed into the cab at two o'clock. "We were planning to be at city hall by noon. Can you imagine a churchful of guests waiting over two hours for the show to get started?"

As they hit the midtown traffic, Meg wondered if the subway would have been smarter after all. Eventually, though, they reached their destination. A young couple fidgeted nervously as they sat on the hard bench and waited their turn to exchange vows. "Only one ahead of us," Amy said. "That's a break."

Twenty minutes later they stood before the Justice of Peace. Jerry and Amy exchanged vows and rings. "By the power invested in me by the State of New York," the J.P. intoned, "I now pronounce you man and wife."

It was not quite the wedding of Meg's dreams, but she felt the lump in her throat just the same. She stole a glance at Brian, who stood on Jerry's right. She saw him brush away a tear and knew that he must be thinking back to his own wedding, thinking back to the hopes that he and Laurie shared, then remembering the accident that killed all of this dreams.

They took turns taking pictures. They enlisted a friendly-looking clerk to shoot a few of the whole wedding party. Finally they hailed two cabs and directed them back to the lower Village and Amy's apartment. This time Amy and Jerry rode together, and the other three adults and Michael took the second taxi.

As they neared their destination, Liz leaned forward and spoke to the cabby. The driver double-parked by a small delicatessen. Liz jumped out and motioned for Brian to follow. They were back in a few minutes with a small feast—platters of pasta, cold cuts, salads, rolls. "I called this morning while Amy was in the shower," Liz said. "She may be too excited to eat, but I knew I'd be starving."

"I insisted that Michael eat a peanut-butter sandwich before we went over to Amy's," Brian said. "Even so, he'll be ready for food by now. The pasta will be just his thing."

They carried the platters upstairs and spread everything out on Amy's coffee table. Meg rummaged in the cupboard for paper plates. Brian opened a bottle of wine that he found in the refrigerator and poured a little for each person. "A toast," he said. "To Mr. and Mrs. Adams, and to the play."

Later, they cut the cake. Amy insisted on tossing her bouquet. She stood on a chair and turned her back to the two eligible females. "First time I've had a fifty-fifty chance at this," Liz quipped. The two women stood right next to each other, but the bouquet made a perfect arc into Meg's outstretched hand.

Meg returned the flowers to Amy, insisting that she wear them as a corsage to the play that night and then press them as a keepsake. She caught Brian staring at her. The color flooded her face as she felt that he could read her thoughts—another wedding, one that definitely involved him.

Liz and Meg volunteered to baby-sit with Michael. The others got ready to head to the theater. Liz tucked something in Amy's hand. "My wedding present," she said.

Amy looked at the piece of paper. "Hotel reservations!" she exclaimed as she hugged Liz.

"For my own comfort," Liz said. "Meg and I didn't feel like sharing Jerry's apartment with Brian and Michael while you two came back here. We'll just keep Michael here with us tonight, Brian. You can collect him in the morning."

"No, I'll come back for him. I'd like to spend some time with you and Meg before you head back tomorrow." He stared at Meg. She tried to interpret his look.

"In that case, we'll take him to Jerry's apartment now. That way we'll get to see you when you get back from the play, and you won't have to wake him up and cart him off with you. The two of us can call a cab to get back here."

Brian nodded, still staring at Meg.

Michael was tucked in, sound asleep after his very busy day. Meg flopped down on Jerry's couch—a new acquisition, she noted. A sure sign that the play was doing well. She kicked off her shoes and tucked her feet under her. Liz was stretched out full length on the floor, her head on one of the oversized pillows. "I suppose this was easier than months of planning," she said.

"Umm," Meg agreed. "Got everything over at once."

"And you're next. You caught the bouquet. Would you prefer months of planning, or would you elope next weekend if he asked?"

Meg had her mouth open to ask who Liz had in mind, but she realized how silly that would sound. "He's not ready," she said. "And I'm not ready either. I'm not ready to fall in love with someone who is still mourning his wife."

"You're kidding yourself," Liz said. "You may not be ready to *marry* him, but it's far too late to protest that you're not ready to fall in love.

If Meg hoped that Brian had planned anything more than casual conversation, she was sorely disappointed. They rehashed the events of the day, all in agreement that it was about as perfect as a spur-of-the-moment wedding could possibly be. They talked about Brian's reaction to the unexpected success of the play, and he said again that it had been fun but that he'd be happy enough to be done with it. "Maybe the touring company, later, if it comes to that," he said in jest. "Maybe summer stock, once it becomes a classic."

Liz was the first to yawn. "Ready?" she asked Meg. "It can always be separate cabs, if you'd like to stay a while."

Meg found the yawn contagious. She covered her mouth with her hand. "I think it's either go with you now or fall asleep here on the couch," she said. She glanced at Brian and caught him in his own yawn. "Liz and I both plan an early start tomorrow," she said. "But we'll see you back in Bennington in, what? . . . three weeks?"

"Something like that. Tony's return date isn't etched in stone."

Liz phoned for the cab. They chattered on for another ten minutes about the wedding while Meg watched out the front window for the taxi. "It's here," she said. Brian pulled himself up from the floor and hugged both women. Meg kissed him on the cheek. Then she and Liz waved good-bye and headed down the stairs to the street.

Chapter Seventeen

Brian's car pulled into the driveway, and Meg ran to meet him. Michael was out of the car in a flash, and greeted Meg with his usual flying tackle around her legs. Brian reached out to steady her, and suddenly she was in his arms.

"Daddy kiss Meg," Michael said.

Oh, yes. Daddy kiss Meg. She wrapped her arms around his neck as her whole being responded to what had started out to be their usual casual kiss.

He stepped back, apparently as surprised as she was. "I'm really glad to be home," he said. He ran a hand through his hair, apparently at a loss for words. "I'm really glad to be back with you," he added.

She grabbed his hand and took Michael's small hand with her other one. "Come on in. We'll scare up some coffee, and milk and cookies."

"Cookies," Michael said.

She bustled around the kitchen, putting the coffee on to brew, getting the cookie jar down from its shelf and putting it on the table. She poured a glass of milk for Michael and got out mugs for herself and Brian. She carefully avoided looking at him, certain that all her feelings would show on her face. She didn't want to seem like a teenager, bowled over by her first real kiss. *It probably meant nothing to him—or he meant it to be nothing, and now he's afraid that I think it's some sort of commitment.*

"We have to talk, Meg."

She looked at him in surprise. *Well,* she thought, *now is when he tells me that he's not ready to be in a serious relationship.*

Michael had finished his milk and cookies and was amusing himself and Fang by dangling a catnip mouse by the tail, holding it just out of the cat's reach. Brian glanced at them, lowered his voice, and continued. "I'm not ready to be in a serious relationship, Meg . . ."

Called that one exactly right, she said to herself. *Word-for-word, even.*

". . . but I guess we can't always pick the time to fall in love." He reached out and took her hand. "I don't know what took me so long to realize how I feel. I love you, Meg. I knew that for sure when we stood with Amy and Jerry and listened to them exchange their vows. But I meant it when I said I wasn't ready for a new relationship. I still haven't come to terms with Laurie's death. I'm afraid to be in love again. It hurts too much when something goes wrong. I'm even scared by how much I love Michael. If anything ever happened to him, I think I'd go out of my mind. I can't ask you to get involved with me now."

Tears sprung to her eyes. She knew that he was right. He wasn't ready for love. But love had come to him uninvited, just as it had come to her. What good would it do to deny it? "I love you too, Brian," she said. "I understand all the problems. Maybe together we can solve them—or at least some of them."

He leaned over and kissed her gently. "Daddy kiss Meg," Michael said.

"Daddy plans on kissing Meg often," Brian said as he pulled her to her feet and kissed her more seriously.

Meg called Liz and asked if she wanted to go out for pizza with them. "I thought Brian wasn't coming home till tomorrow," Liz said. "I thought we were having dinner at your house then."

"We can still do that. I thought it was tomorrow, too. He surprised me too, Liz." Meg glanced at Brian as she realized "he surprised me" was an enormous understatement. "So—pick you up in ten minutes?"

Brian held Meg's hand as they drove to Liz's place. She must have been watching from her apartment window, because she was down the stairs before Brian rang the doorbell. He opened the rear car door for her, and she slid in next to Michael.

"Daddy kiss Meg," Michael said, as if he could hardly wait to spread the news.

"Well. Tell me more."

The comment was directed to all of them, but only Michael answered. "Daddy kiss Meg *often*." He emphasized the last word, a new one for him.

"You're a good source of information, Michael. Not

too great on the details, but just fine with the bare facts." She leaned toward the front seat. "Anybody want to add anything?"

"We don't have any announcements to make, if that's what you're fishing for, Liz."

"I think I'd know if we were talking about an engagement, Brian. And I didn't think you were moving in with her."

Meg felt that she should say something. "I guess we'll see how being a couple works for us. This is pretty new, Liz. We haven't been holding out on you."

"New, like last hour or so," Brian added.

"And you're celebrating by going out for pizza with Michael and me? Doesn't sound real romantic."

"Pizza, pizza!" Michael bounced a little in his car seat. "Hungry!"

"Does that answer your question?" Brian asked. "We have to feed Mike. It seemed sensible to see if our best friend in town was hungry too."

Brian and Meg were at his house, snuggled next to each other on the couch, enjoying the blazing fire. Michael was tucked into bed, tired from an afternoon of running with Brandy in the field behind Meg's house.

Brian and Meg were tired, too, and comfortable without conversation. Off and on they shared a kiss that turned Meg's legs to jelly. "I never knew it could be like this," she whispered. When he didn't answer, she said, "This is really the first time for me. I know you've been in love before and I know you'll never forget Laurie. I think it's wonderful that you've been blessed by more than one love."

* * *

Meg knew, as soon as she awoke, even before she looked out the window. There was something about the light, about the quiet, that told her that there had been a major snowfall. Well, this was to be expected. The "onion snow," the old-timers called it—the April snowfall that they waited for, knowing that until it came and then melted they dared not set out the tender onion flats. It was late this year, nearly the middle of April instead of during the first week. Already a few daffodils had forced their way out of the ground, and, as always, folks had begun to think that this year they might miss this final storm.

The phone rang. "Tobogganing?" Brian asked. "I have this small child here who is begging, and I know that Thursday's not a teaching day for you."

"Do I get breakfast first?"

"How about we stop at Denny's? That will make it a doubly special day for Mike."

"In that case you can pick me up in ten minutes. I can let Brandy out for a run while I get dressed. I have the animals fed by the time you arrive."

It was just the right kind of snow for the toboggan—wet and heavy as opposed to light and fluffy. Meg knew the best hill, a fairly steep slope at the foothills of a real mountain. Holmes Hill didn't look quite as big as she remembered from her childhood, but Michael's gasp as they stood staring up to the top put its size back in perspective. They started up the slope. Meg wondered how many treks they would be able to make.

They tucked Michael between them and pushed off from the top. It felt like flying. Meg couldn't remember when she'd done anything so exciting, anything that made her feel so free. The icy air whipped by her face, leaving it chapped and raw. Each bump reverberated through her spine, and she knew that she would be stiff and sore next day. But she was in her element, and could hardly wait to climb back up the mountain and ride back down again.

Up they climbed again, and down they flew. "For a Southern boy, you're pretty good at this," Meg said as they trudged up the hill for the third time.

"I learned just last year. Jason was taking Robbie, so of course I got roped into bringing Michael and going along. Jason taught me to steer. I never knew that you had to steer. I thought you just pointed the toboggan towards the bottom of the hill and let 'er rip."

Meg laughed. "With this hill that would probably work. On hills with trees, it's best to be with someone who knows how to steer."

For the fourth trek up, Brian carried Michael on his shoulders. Mike kept saying "more toboggan," but the little legs were just about worn out.

After the fifth run down the hill, even Michael was ready to go home for hot chocolate and a peanut butter sandwich. His cheeks were rosy and his nose was running. Meg was willing to bet that he'd be ready for a nap after lunch, even though he'd told her many times that he was "way too old for naps." Meg stretched her aching legs and thought that maybe even she wouldn't be too old for a nap that afternoon.

Chapter Eighteen

Meg was awakened by the phone. The steely light that came in the bedroom window told her that the onion snow still lay thick and heavy on the ground. She reached for the phone, then sat bolt upright as the words filtered through her sleep-logged brain. "Michael's missing!" Brian yelled.

"Calm down," she said, knowing that there was no way for that to happen. "Tell me what happened."

"He got up and fixed himself some cereal. He often does that. I leave the milk in a little pitcher in the fridge so that he can pour it himself. I know I should see that he eats a proper breakfast—"

She interrupted. "Brian, the breakfast doesn't matter. Not right now."

"Right. He's wearing his snowsuit and boots. Even his mittens."

168

"Then maybe he's right outside, rolling around in the snow."

"I looked, Meg. I shouted for him. Jason and Angela are searching the neighborhood right now."

"Go and help them," Meg said. "I'll get into my ski clothes and come right over." She hung up the phone and hurried into her foul-weather outfit. "Come on, Brandy," she called as she headed out the door.

Even as she backed out of the driveway Meg had started to imagine the worst. It was, despite the heavy snowfall, nearly spring. The ice on the ponds would be thin; skating would be over for the year. *But Michael won't know that. I promised to take him skating here, in Bennington, on the pond behind the college. Suppose he is even now under the ice, turning colder. I should never have taken him skating in New York. I should never have made it seem like such fun.*

She made a U-turn and drove back the way she'd come, headed now to the college and the pond just beyond. She drove into the college's main road, up past the Barn and the Commons, past the library and the dorms. She parked in the lot next to the science building. She walked back through the woods until she came to a small clearing. The snow lay thick on the pond, with no small footprints disturbing its pristine surface. She breathed a sigh of relief.

She pulled into Brian's driveway and he ran to meet her from a block or two down the street. "Where have you been?" he yelled. She started to explain, but he cut her off. "I just found out that he was spotted by some people five blocks over," he said. He waved his arm in the general direction of the mountains. "He was already too far away to recognize, halfway up Holmes Hill when they saw the red snowsuit against the snow. They called the police. They've been combing the area for an hour. So far, no luck."

"Let's go," Meg said. "Get something of Michael's for Brandy to sniff. I don't know how she is at tracking, but it won't hurt to try.

"That's where we were yesterday," she said as Brian came out with Michael's pajamas. "Do you suppose he went back there?"

"That's what I'm thinking. Maybe he thought he could slide down the hill on his rear, *sans* toboggan." He slid into the passenger seat and Meg took off for Holmes Hill.

Somehow she had expected to see the little red-snowsuited figure right away. Instead she saw the hill crawling with police and other searchers. Now she had to think about whether Michael had changed his mind, gone somewhere else before the police arrived. Or climbed higher? How far could a three-year-old get?

The mountain loomed beyond its small foothill. Meg remembered how Michael had stared up at it the day before. "Do you think he's up there?" she asked, gazing up at the forbidding heights.

"We sure can't add much to the activity here. I'll talk to Chief Burns and tell him that we're climbing up. Got your hiking boots on?"

She nodded. "Maybe a few others will come with us. It's a big mountain."

She followed Brian as he headed up the hill towards the Chief of Police. "We'll take the north face," she heard him say, "if some of your men can go up the south trail."

"I'm going to send most of these people to scope out the rest of the countryside," the chief said. "He's sure not on this foothill."

"I've already checked the pond behind Bennington's science building," Meg said. Brian looked abashed, and she knew he was sorry he'd yelled at her for taking so long to reach him.

"He may have climbed the mountain," Chief Burns said, "but he may have just turned around and headed . . . who knows where? We saw some footprints when we first got here, but the wind had already wiped out most of them. And now it's blowing so hard that there's no way to follow the trail. Is someone your house in case he finds his way home while we're searching for him?"

"No, but his daily care person lives next door. Angela promised to watch for him. He'd most likely go to her house if he came home and discovered I wasn't there. And Angela promised to check every hour or so. She'd find him even if he just walked in the house and crawled into bed and fell asleep."

Burns nodded. He headed off to organize the search party, casting the net wider than Holmes Hill.

"Ready?" Brian set his eye on the mountain.

Meg stared up at the sky. The air seemed heavy and filled with foreboding. *But we had the onion snow, last night*, she told herself. *Two storms in April are unheard of.* She bit her lip. They needed good visibility, for their own safety as well as for finding the child.

They stood at the top of Holmes Hill. Only yesterday they had sledded down to where the searchers were now climbing into cars and trucks, heading off in every direction. Meg and Brian turned in the other direction, gazing at the steep rise of the mountain. "Think he could have climbed it?" she asked.

"He climbed this far yesterday. Two or three times, before I started carrying him up on my shoulders. He wouldn't have had any trouble getting to foot of the mountain; there's just that little dip and then a level stretch, and then he'd be ready to head up the trail to the top."

"Let's go, Brian." She glanced at the sky again. She didn't want to put her worries into words.

The wind during the night had blown much of the snow from the trail, so Meg and Brian found that the hike was not too difficult. Meg wondered whether that was good news or bad. The easier the climb, the more likely that a determined three-year-old could manage it.

The dog ran in circles, unable to pick up a scent. She raced ahead, then back to Meg and Brian. The wind still howled around the mountain, ensuring that any small footprints would be long gone.

They paused at the first turnoff and looked in all directions. Brandy ran back and forth, waiting to see where they went next. "He could be anywhere," Brian said in despair.

"We'll find him," Meg said as she grabbed his hand. "The whole town is searching for him." She looked around again. "What do you think? Stay on the main trail?"

"Yes. If he really came this way, he'd be making a bee-line for the summit. That's what we'll do too."

Brandy and Brian were still full of energy by the time they reached the level area that Meg knew was at the halfway point, but she was a little winded. She tried to compare her abilities to Michael's. She began to wonder if he could possibly have come this far. Still, the mountain seemed a likely place for him to be. Could they have missed him? Could he have taken one of the side trails? Could he have sat down to rest? How quickly might a small child lose body heat in this weather if he stopped moving? Meg fought her weariness, fought the beginnings of despair.

The first snowflakes began to fall, fat and heavy. Brandy ran in circles again, but then she stood still, yapped loudly, and headed up the trail. Her nose twitched, and she held it close to the ground. "I think she smells something," Meg said.

"Probably a squirrel, or whatever kind of animal is crazy enough to live up here. But I don't have any better ideas, so we might as well follow her. I don't like this weather, though. If this keeps up, there could be more than one person lost on this mountain."

"Lead on, Brandy," Meg yelled. She took a deep breath and followed the dog. *We have to find him*, she said to herself. *Another tragedy would be more than Brian could bear.* She couldn't even imagine it. To lose a wife and unborn child and then, later, to lose the son how had become his whole life?

Chapter Nineteen

As they reached the mountain's summit the snow began falling heavily. The wind picked up, swirling the white flakes nearly sideways. The fat flakes had been replaced by icy needles. "Visibility is down to almost nothing," Brian shouted, trying to make himself heard above the howling wind. "Who would have thought that a storm like this could come up so quickly?" He cupped his hand around his mouth and yelled. "Michael! Where are you?" The mountains sent back the echo, but there was no answer from his small son. Brian shouted in each direction, sending his plea out over the rugged hills.

Brandy was still sniffing, but Meg knew that the trail was growing cold as the snow began to accumulate. The big dog ran in circles as she tried to catch the child's scent.

The hours passed. She wondered if they walked in

174

circles. Meg began to fear that they might find the child too late, or that they too might die on the mountain. Only the dog seemed warm as she ran from one snowy outcrop to another, still trying to track the lost child. Meg stomped her feet and blew on her frozen fingers.

"If we stay much longer, there will be three bodies instead of one," Brian said. His exhaustion showed on his face.

"He's not dead. I know he's not dead. And he needs us, Brian. We can't give up now."

"I can't go on," Brian said. He sat down on the snow.

She went to him, concern showing on her face. "Are you hurt?"

He shook his head. "I can't go on because I have no hope."

In truth, she was near to it. "Everyone feels despair at some time in his life," she said. "But you can't let it become a part of you. You have to fight it."

"I can't fight it. I have no fight left." The tears ran down Brian's cheeks, freezing into icy furrows. She held him while he cried; she rocked back and forth as she would with a child. "Let the tears come," she said. "Let go. Let it out—the hurt and the fear and the suffering."

He stayed locked in her arms for what seemed like hours as he sobbed over his wife's death, over the unborn baby, over this new tragedy. The snow swirled around them. Meg felt as if she were frozen to the ground.

A glint of sunshine broke through the clouds over the mountain, and the still-falling snow sparkled like a million diamonds. From somewhere on the other side of the summit on which they knelt they heard a whimper, the sound magnified strangely in the thin mountain air. Brandy's ears perked up, and she was over the top and out of sight before Meg and Brian could get to their feet. Brian's face showed his hope, the first in a long time.

The big Saint Bernard was digging frantically. Then she stopped, sat back on her haunches, and whimpered. Brian and Meg ran to the place where she'd been digging. They saw the problem right away. Brandy had uncovered a deep crevasse. It seemed to run clear to the center of the earth. "Michael!" Brian yelled as he leaned into the hole. His voice echoed off the walls of the fissure.

From a long way off came the answering call. "Daddy! Daddy! I can't get out!"

"We'll have to go down there," Meg said.

Brian looked at her as if she'd lost her mind. "Even if we could get down there, we'd never get out. It's pointless anyway." He glanced down at his body, Santa-like in the heavy snow gear. "I won't fit."

"I will," Meg countered. "Michael is frightened, Brian. And maybe hurt. And maybe it isn't as deep as we think. It seems to bend around a little; maybe that's why his voice sounds so far away. I have to go to him. If it's as deep as you say, maybe at least I can keep him warm while you go for more help—and ropes."

"If I have to go back to town, you'll both freeze before I get back," he said. He looked up at the sky. "Sun's setting. Temperature will drop thirty or forty degrees in the next couple of hours."

"Chief Burns and his crew should be coming up the south trail," she said.

"That takes nearly twice as long as coming up this side. And I don't remember that they had ropes."

"Then we'll have to manage by ourselves." She walked over to the crack in the earth and sat down beside it, lowering her feet into the hole. "Take my hands," she said. "Lie on your stomach, and we'll see if maybe I don't have too far to drop."

She scooted over the side. She felt as if her arms would pop out of the shoulder sockets when she made the drop. She gritted her teeth and grimaced at the pain. Brian held fast to her hands. Her feet swung free.

No light penetrated the crevasse, so she had no idea how far it was to the bottom. "Michael!" she yelled.

The answer came from the left, and seemingly not too far away. She'd been right in thinking that the fissure didn't run straight down. She let go of Brian with her left hand, wincing as that threw all of her weight onto her right shoulder. She reached out with her free hand and touched the wall. She whispered a prayer and let go of Brian.

It was maybe a four-foot drop. She twisted her ankle, but nothing seemed to be broken. She called to Michael, and he found her in the dark and clung to her. "We're going to try to get you up on my shoulders," she said, even as she felt around her prison and wondered how they could manage in such a confined space. "Do you know how to do that? I'll make a step out of my hands, and you'll put your foot on it, and I'll lift you up. Put your hands on the walls of this hole to steady yourself. When you get your feet on my shoulders, try to stand up as straight as you can. Hold your hands up high. I think your daddy will be able to grab you."

The space was dark and cramped, but eventually she managed to get Michael into the proper position. "I can see daylight," the little boy said happily. "But I think the dark will be here soon." He stood up, balancing himself with one hand against the walls of their prison. He reached toward his father with his other hand.

"I can't quite reach," Brian yelled. "I need another six inches. If I scoot forward much further on my stomach I'll loose my leverage."

"Inch forward, Brian," she yelled. To the child she said, "Stretch as high as you can, Michael. Stand on your toes." She stood up on her own toes as well as she could in the heavy snow boots.

"I've got him," Brian yelled, and Meg felt the weight lifted off her shoulders—literally as well as figuratively.

She was not surprised that it took a few moments for the reunion to take place. She could hear the happy Saint Bernard running back and forth, woofing with delight. She waited patiently in her prison until Brian finally yelled down the hole, "Now what? You don't have anyone's shoulders to stand on, Meg."

"Maybe I can . . . what do you call it? . . . you know, when a mountain climber just puts his back on one side of the fissure and his feet on the other and shimmies his way up. Is that rappelling?"

"I don't know. I think rappelling involves ropes, which is what we need right now. Whatever it's called, do you know how to do it?"

"Only in theory." She tried to wedge herself between the walls of the crevasse. "It isn't going to work, Brian," she said after a few minutes. "I twisted my ankle when I dropped down here, and I can't put enough pressure on it."

"We need a rope." Meg's heart sank. She was certain she'd freeze to death before Brian could get in to town and back with the necessary supplies. "Take off your snowpants," she heard him say.

"But Daddy, it's too cold."

"I need them, Michael. I'm going to tie one leg of yours to one leg of mine. I think that will make a long enough rope." Meg tried to picture the scene as she waited. "Nope," Brian said. We'll need my jeans as well."

She looked up gratefully to see the rather strange rescue device that descended towards her. She grabbed it with both hands and found that she could put one foot over another along the wall, gradually making her ascent. As her head cleared the opening, she was treated to a sight that she would never forget. Brian, Michael, and the dog were all holding onto the tied-together pants. Brian had tied his jacket around his waist, evidently feeling that his nearly bare lower regions needed the warmth more than his ski-sweatered arms and torso.

Meg stepped out of the crevasse, and Brian enfolded her in his arms. "Snowpants, Daddy," came a small voice. "Cold."

They untied their clothing, and Meg turned her back while Brian got all pairs of pants back on. She felt that he deserved his privacy, but it also gave her a chance to laugh without being obscrved. She knew that for the rest of her life, whenever she needed a chuckle, she would conjure up the vision of the partially clothed man, the boy, and the dog all engaged in what looked like an old-time tug-o'-war as they pulled her out of the crevasse.

And then she was back in his arms, crying and laughing at the same time. He kissed her then, a promise of more to come. He looked at the sky. "Getting dark," he said, "and about to snow another two, three feet. Can you hobble on that foot if you lean on me?"

Chapter Twenty

It was meant to be a simple wedding in the meadow, but the number of participants grew and grew. Michael, of course, would carry the rings. John's five-year-old daughter would be flower girl. Liz would be maid of honor, but Julia and Sally and Amy and Angela refused to be left out. Jerry was best man. John was tapped to give away the bride.

The wildflowers of early spring—gentians and columbine and lily-of-the-valley and pussy willow—filled the meadow and made up the bouquets carried by the women in their simple summer dresses. Vases at the foot of the makeshift altar were filled to overflowing with forsythia and apple blossoms and lilacs. The air was heavy with their perfume. Meg was in a long white dress of cotton eyelet, her veil was held in place by a circlet of hawthorn blossoms that she'd picked that morning.

181

Meg turned to Brian and took his hand as she reached the altar. She saw tears in his eyes. She knew he would never forget Laurie, but she knew that he was ready to build their new life together.

Meg and Brian spoke together as they made their vows. "I Margaret take thee Brian," she said, "to be my wedded husband. To have and to hold from this day forward, for better, for worse, for richer, for poorer, in sickness and in health, to love and to cherish, till death us do part."

They exchanged rings, saying together, "In token and pledge of the vow between us made, with this ring I thee wed."

Brian kissed Meg lightly. They made their way back through the wildflowers of the meadow, followed by their friends and relatives and the gamboling cat and dog, toward the house where all would gather to toast the beginnings of their lives together.

Fulton Co. Public Library
320 W. 7th St.
Rochester, IN 46975